DEDICATION

This book is dedicated to the memory of my grandfather,
Joseph Dynan,
soldier and story-teller.

CONTENTS

ACKNOWLEDGMENTS

My thanks to Jeremy Meadows who designed the poppy icon used in this book. Thanks also to John and the staff at 'picnic' in Reading for sustaining me with copious cups of coffee while I worked and fostering a little creative haven in the heart of the town. Most especially, my thanks to my partner, ML, who has supported me throughout and believed in me always.

The Maiwand Lion

"This monument commemorates the names and records the valour and devotion of 11 officers and 318 non-commissioned officers and men of the 66th Berkshire Regiment who gave their lives for their country at Girishk, Maiwand and Kandahar during the Afghan Campaign 1878-1880."

These are the words inscribed on the plinth of the Maiwand Lion, a massive cast-iron sculpture and war memorial found in Forbury Gardens, a public park in the town of Reading, Berkshire in England. It honours the memory of British soldiers killed in action in Afghanistan in the latter part of the nineteenth century and was unveiled in December 1886. The Berkshire Regiment lost over half its men at the bloody battle of Maiwand where it faced an Afghan army many times larger. Such was the courage and bravery of these men that they were honoured by their enemies.

This was Britain's last major military campaign in Afghanistan until the war of 2001, following the attack on the United States of America on September 11th that year by terrorists based there. At the time of writing, over 400 British military personnel have lost their lives in this operation and many more have been seriously injured, physically and psychologically.

CHAPTER ONE

Remembrance Sunday, November 2009, Reading, Berkshire.

I don't remember really seeing it before that morning, not properly anyway, although it's hard to imagine that now, this huge iron statue of a lion standing on top of a plinth, proud and roaring, protecting its domain, defiant. I remember just standing there, looking up at it, sleek with rain, on a cold grey November morning. Ash sidled up to me.

'You OK?' he asked, slightly awkwardly.

'Yeah, fine, y'know. Just didn't feel like mixing with the crowd 'til I have to.'

I nodded towards the people gathering around the entrance to the Forbury Gardens, around the War Memorial. They wore uniforms some of them, military uniforms many of them, but some school uniforms, like mine. Everyone wore a red poppy in their coat lapels, men and women, for Remembrance Sunday. It was the first time I'd attended one of these events ever, if I'm honest. But today I'd been given a 'special honour', as Mr. Brennan put it, and would lay the poppy wreath on behalf of the school. They'd asked Mr. Brennan to ask me if I'd be alright with this, and he told me they'd understand perfectly if I felt I couldn't do it, given the circumstances, if I found it too 'upsetting'. He looked embarrassed when he talked to me then, which was unusual for him, normally so 'well composed', as Gran would say. I thought it 'ironic' (my new favourite word back then) that an English teacher could find it so hard to find the right words to say to me. But then, everyone had been awkward around me about that time, since, y'know, my Dad died. Or was killed, I should say. By the Taliban. In Afghanistan. By one of their road-side bombs. IEDs, my Dad use to call them, when he talked about his work, 'improvised explosive devices'. This made them seem a bit crap, like something amateurish, like something we'd make in science class. Those volcano-type experiments we did in First Year, with baking soda and stuff. Like that, a bit naff, not too serious. No match for armoured cars and bomb-disposal equipment and body armour and stuff. That's what my Dad did, he was a bomb disposal expert. Before he died, anyway. Before he was killed, murdered, by the Taliban and their crappy bombs. Killed, right there, in the road, last August. Barely three months ago, now. That's why people were awkward around me. The school teachers as well as my mates. Except for Ash, he just persisted. He just carried on. Not as if nothing had happened, as such, more like he wanted me to be 'normal' with him. But we were both far from normal anyway, even before all this stuff. Geeks, nerds, swots and outsiders. That's how we felt. But we didn't really mind being different. Liked it, really. 'Ye don't want to be a sheep, anyway, do ye?' Gran always said. But Dad would have preferred it if I'd loved football, like he did, or boxing or stuff like that. But I didn't, don't. I think he still liked me, though. I know that it wasn't my fault he broke up with Mum. They both told me that. It was just that his job made it hard for Mum to live her life the way she wanted, and she wanted what was best for me, too. A good school, a good education. I wanted to become a doctor, like my Uncle Edward. And I needed to stay in one place long enough to get a good education. And Mum had family here in Reading, Uncle Edward and Gran. So we came here, about three years ago, when I was twelve. And I started secondary school here. And Dad lived with the Army. And went to Iraq and then Afghanistan. And then he died, was killed, by the Taliban.

Ash was looking up at the lion now, too. He was looking at the lion's mouth, squinting his eyes through his glasses, which had little drops of water on them, from the light drizzle which was falling.

'It's a war memorial, too, y'know,' he said. 'From one of the previous Afghan Wars.' He looked at me to see if I reacted, but I didn't, on purpose. 'It's all here on the plinth, at the side, see. I read about it on Wikipedia, too. It's called the "Maiwand Lion" after some village in Afghanistan where the British fought against an Afghan army ten times as big, or something like that, anyway. Loads of them were killed but their enemies were so impressed by their bravery that they honoured them.'

'Are you sure that wasn't "Zulu Dawn"?' I asked sarcastically.

'No, look, it's written here on the side.' He tugged my arm slightly to wheel me around to the side of the plinth where a bronze plaque was inscribed with a dedication. He started to read it out loud:

"This monument commemorates the names and records the valour and devotion of (he paused for a second to decipher the Roman numerals written to represent the numbers) 11 officers and (a longer pause then as he tried again to decipher the numbers) 318 non-commissioned officers and men of the 66th Berkshire Regiment who gave their lives for their country at Girishk Maiwand and Kandahar during the Afghan Campaign 1878-1880. 'History does not afford any grander or finer instance of gallantry and devotion to Queen and country than that displayed by the 66th Regiment at the Battle of Maiwand on the 27th July 1880': Despatch of General Primrose." See, I told you, and there's more on Wikipedia, too.'

'Really, Ash, you do surprise me?' I replied wearily.

'Did you know that Sir Arthur Conan Doyle based the character of Dr. Watson on the Regiment's medical officer, 'cos he was so brave, and stuff?'

'I always thought Watson was a bit of a wuss,' I sneered.

'Well, no actually, if you read the novels he's quite brave and intelligent. They're releasing a new movie about Sherlock Holmes around Christmas and apparently he's quite, er, dashing.'

'Dashing?!' I guffawed. 'Where the hell did you hear a word like that. You sound like Brennan spouting about the Romantic poets!'

Ash shifted awkwardly. He didn't like to be teased, especially as it happened so often. I instantly regretted my words so tried to cheer him up.

'Sorry, that's really interesting. I didn't know about any of that. I didn't really appreciate how long ago we'd been involved in Afghanistan, actually.'

'Well, that wasn't the last time, either,' Ash started off again enthusiastically. 'The Third Afghan War happened just after World War One and the RAF bombed Kabul, then. But there weren't really many British troops in Afghanistan again until, well, recently...' Ash's voice faded off, realising that he was approaching a sensitive subject. 'Anyway, I just thought you might find it interesting to know, that's all.'

'No, it is, interesting,' I said. 'Interesting that we've been having British troops killed there in that shit-hole since Victoria was on the throne and we still do, today.' Ash flinched at the use of the swear words and looked down at his shoes. We both stood silently for a while. Then Mr. Brennan came walking up the short gravel path from the War Memorial to the Lion, calling to us to get our attention.

'Andrew, Ash!' He did that sort of walk-run thing older people do when they're trying to get a move on but feel it's beneath their dignity to run outright. He was pulling his dark woollen overcoat around him as he trotted towards us, a red poppy on his collar like a splash of blood. He was obviously wearing his 'Sunday best'. He was slightly out of breath when he reached us. I could smell coffee on his breath as he stood before us.

'We're nearly ready to begin. I saw your Mum a few minutes ago, Andrew. I'm sure this is a difficult day for you both.' He smiled weakly at me and touched my shoulder lightly, trying to be reassuring, I'm sure but coming off a bit creepy. Ash looked away, feeling like he was intruding into something private.

'We were just talking about the lion, here,' I said quickly, looking up towards the dark grey iron mass above our heads. Brennan looked up, too, slightly abashed at having been dismissed by me like that. 'Quite interesting, really. It's a war memorial from the last time we were in Afghanistan, did you know that?'

'Yes, I did, actually. It was sculpted by a chap called Simonds, one of the brewing family, you know, Simonds Brewery. There's a story that he committed suicide following criticism of the stance of the lion, which people said was based on that of a domestic cat rather than the "king of the jungle". But, as Mark Twain once said, the rumours of his death were much exaggerated and he actually lived to a ripe old age, running the family business.' He smiled weakly, thinking I'd be impressed or something. This was the closest Brennan got to humour, quoting some old long-dead 'wit', as he'd call them, in class. We all remained staring up at the lion for a second or two, not knowing really what else to say to each other. Then Brennan said we should get back to the War Memorial as the ceremony was about to begin shortly. We walked over to the entrance to the Forbury Gardens, to where everyone was gathered, chatting among themselves, slightly hushed, like in a church. I noticed people looking at me, some whispering among some old biddies, probably saying that I was the one who's Dad had been killed. I felt like I just wanted to keep on walking and then I saw Mum. She was with Uncle Edward and Gran, all dressed up in her best work suit, black pin-stripe with a black silk blouse underneath. She also wore a hat, with a little veil, a bit over the top, if you asked me. But Gran insisted it would 'add to the dignity of the occasion.' She herself wore her black wool coat with the fur trim collar (fake, of course), with a fur hat to match. She looked like a little Russian babushka, instead of the old Irish woman she really was. And Uncle Edward, of course, looked like he always did, well-polished, dignified and concerned. He had an arm from each of them looped around his, protectively. Suddenly, they all noticed me, and all smiled at me.

'Sure, here he is, the star of the show,' Gran said, reaching an arm out to pat me on the shoulder. 'Doesn't he look grand in his school uniform? Your Dad would be proud...' Her voice suddenly trailed off, caught with emotion. Her eyes were moist and glistened in the low winter sunlight.

'Are you all set, then, Andrew? ' Uncle Edward jumped in, saving us from further emotion.

'Yeah, I'm fine. I just need to find the wreath and then I'm good to go!'

'Yes, the wreath', Mr. Brennan interjected, 'One of my colleagues is holding onto it for me over there. Let's go, Andrew, and get into position. We'll catch up with your family after the ceremony.' He smiled his goodbyes and shuffled me over to where a small knot of kids from my school were gathered. Natasha smiled at me as I came over.

'You OK?' she asked, in a slightly maternal way, like she was looking after me or something. I didn't mind, really. Natasha was nice and one of the few female friends I had. She touched my shoulder, too, when she spoke. Seemed like everyone was doing that today. If we were American, she would have hugged me, like they do in 'Friends'. But we were British and slightly awkward, so we just smiled and joked.

'Yeah, cool,' I said. 'Looking forward to getting this all over with, to be honest. It's bloody freezing here, this morning.'

Next thing I heard was the sudden blast of music from the brass instruments of the Army Band, who led a small colour party the short distance from St. Laurence's Church, where the service had been conducted a little time before. The crowd all turned their heads towards the group of soldiers, marching stiffly towards us, various regimental flags moving slightly as they walked through the light drizzle, no wind though. An air of formality suddenly descended, as they came close by and started to parade on the little Forbury Square. A sergeant major or something started to yell some orders, and the little group came to attention. They then started to present their flags, holding them at an angle so that they unfurled, letting us see the various insignias and colours more clearly. Then the Reverend started to speak through the microphone and the crappy sound system, which made his voice sound far away, like it wasn't coming out of his mouth. He asked us to observe a silence as a mark of respect for those who had fallen in all the wars and conflicts which had protected our freedom. The bells of the nearby Town Hall clock tower started to chime, just like Big Ben, and then struck eleven o'clock. Everyone stood still and remained silent. It was weird. Standing there, among so many people, all quiet. I could hear breathing all around me, and even someone's stomach gurgling. I could hear the sound of traffic in the distance. I could even hear a siren some way off, probably near the Royal Berkshire Hospital. But mainly I heard silence and it felt weird, all my friends and classmates around me and me, just standing there. I remember thinking, god, how long do we have to stand like this? It seemed to go on forever. But then, a bugler started playing that song, the Last Post, or whatever, like you hear in the movies. It sounded sad and lonely and despite myself, I found I had to keep swallowing to try to keep down an urge to cry or something. I think they might have played that at Dad's funeral, thinking about it, so maybe that's what set me off.

The Reverend's disembodied voice suddenly broke the silence left when the bugle stopped, saying that there would now follow the laying of the wreaths. Mr. Brennan suddenly appeared at my side, whispering into my ear, which felt a bit disconcerting. He pushed something into my hands. It took me a second or two to realise what he was doing. It was the poppy wreath, the one I had agreed to place at the War Memorial, a stump of granite that looked like a blasted limb. I became aware that other people, older people in uniforms and even the Mayor, I think, were already processing up and down to lay wreaths. I watched them as if they were on TV or something, like I wasn't really there. I saw how they approached the monument, stiffly and formally, how they bent their knee to place the wreath, how they bowed solemnly and waited a moment, as if in quiet contemplation of the 'horrors of war'. Then I became aware of the Reverend's voice, again, speaking as if he was down a well, saying my school's name, then saying my name, saying something about my Dad, and the people, suddenly looking at me, with that look in their eyes, sympathy or pity or something else. Some old biddies were whispering to each other, looking at me. And my Mum, and Gran and Uncle Edward, were looking at me. Uncle Edward seemed to nod to me, smiled encouragingly, as if to nudge me on. Then Brennan, in my ear again:

'OK, Andrew, you're up.'

I moved forward, the wreath in my hands, banging against my knees as I slowly approached the monument. I looked for a space, somewhere to place the thing, stupid thing, why did I agree to do this stupid thing! I found one, to the side, and placed it there, propped up against the granite step, like I'd seen the others do it. And I stood there, for a moment, like the others did, 'contemplating the horrors of war', aware of all those eyes on me, aware too that my eyes were filling up, how did that happen! I was feeling fine a second or two ago and now here I was, brimming over, like a wuss. I suddenly felt like I had to get out of there. I darted back towards the group of class-mates, at the side, looking only at my feet as I made the few strides to rejoin them. I remember thinking, don't look at their faces and don't let them see yours. I took my place again and looked forward, trying not to look at anyone in particular. A warm hand touched mine. I looked down and saw Natasha's hand, squeezing mine. I looked into her face, and she smiled at me, like she was being kind, which, of course, she was. I sort of smiled weakly, and shrugged my shoulders, for some reason, as if to say it was all a bit of a mystery to me. Brennan whispered in my ear again.

'Well done, Andrew. You did us proud, you did your family proud'.

'Thanks, Sir,' I replied, aware of the break in my voice.

I glanced over towards where my Mum was standing. She seemed to be crying, dabbing at her eyes with a white hanky my Uncle Edward had given to her. It was all a bit too 'Hollywood' for me, the grieving widow act! She'd not spoken to him for months before he'd died, been killed, murdered. Now she was standing there, with all these people around her, comforting her for 'her loss', being the star of the show, like she was the only one in pain. She'd lost a husband she'd given up anyway years ago. I'd lost my Dad, my only Dad, whom no one could replace, ever, even if she wanted them to. I felt myself getting angry, clenching my fists, which were now by my side, as I stood, ramrod straight, like I'd seen my Dad do on parade, when I was a little boy, trying to keep it all together. I decided it was better not to look at Mum any more, in case I lost it altogether, which would not do, not here, in front of everyone. I remember I looked away, and noticed that the Maiwand Lion was directly in my line of sight. From this angle, he stood with his body pointing towards me, his forelegs pointing forward, and his head with its massive mane of metal looking out, in profile. I remember thinking I'd just focus on this, while the ceremony ran its course, that this would keep me safe and in control, like the lion. I remember all of those things going through my mind and that it seemed to help, at first anyway. The sounds around me started to fade into the background. I began to feel like I was watching this scene as if it was in a movie, like I was an observer, not a participant. The world seemed to contract, like time slowed down or something. Then the strange taste came in my mouth, something metallic, like blood or something. And then I noticed the dryness at the back of my throat, as if I was parched. I remember trying to swallow but having no spit, just this taste, this strange taste, like blood, in my mouth. Then the smell came, strange smell, not like anything I'd smelt before. No, though, that's not true, it was strange but familiar at the same time. Acrid, if that's the right word. It got right up my nostrils; I could almost taste it too, mixed with the blood. I remember then the grittiness in my mouth, like when you're at the beach and you get sand in your sandwiches which you don't notice until you're crunching down on the grains mixed in with the jam, that feeling of something crunching between your teeth, alien and unexpected. I remember then the weird feeling in my head, the sense of lightheadedness, like when you're in an aircraft and it suddenly drops through a pocket of turbulence or something, like the world has dropped away from beneath your feet, like you're standing on the edge of a very tall building, peering over the edge, looking down, like vertigo- if that's what vertigo means. And then the sounds came, not coming from my ears, but from inside my head; the sound like thunder in the distance, or a heavy truck trundling across a metal bridge. I swear, I could even feel the vibrations in my feet, as if the ground was trembling, as if we were having a little earthquake here, in Reading, on a Sunday morning, Remembrance Sunday. I thought other people must surely notice these things, the noise, the smells. I looked around, but it was like I was underwater or something, everything slowed down. All the movements I made felt like I was made of lead, heavy, slow and not able to move except by immense force of will. No one seemed to notice, they were all doing exactly what they'd been doing before this began, all looking forward, towards the War Memorial, all listening to the service. I felt apart from them, like I'd slipped away but was still there. I looked again towards the Maiwand Lion, like I expected somehow that he understood what was happening to me. My eyes started to fill with tears, at least that's what I thought initially when the image before me began to swim, when the edges became blurred, like I was looking through water, light refracted and reflected like when I swam underwater on holidays that time in Spain, with my Dad. I held my breath, like I was swimming; maybe I was, drowning here on dry land. I could feel my heart beating in my chest, thumping, like I could really feel it, like something was trapped inside me, trying to get out, to escape. And I continued to look at the Maiwand Lion, his great grey head profiled against the low leaden skies of November in Reading, with weak winter sunlight filtered through a blanket of low grey rainclouds, drizzling light rain on the crowd assembled here to remember the dead. And then the lion moved, or rather his mane moved, his metal mane cast from iron over a century before, began to move, as if stirred by wind blowing into his face. And then his face moved. His maw of a mouth, opened in a silent roar for over a hundred years, began to move, first his tongue, then his lips and jaw. His whole head was moving, full of

13

movement, his eyes flinching against the wind blowing in his face, stirring his mane. I suddenly noticed his tail swishing behind him, like he was agitated, or preparing to move. Was he preparing to move, to leap from his plinth where he'd stood frozen for an age? Was he now going to leap from his platform, to run free of constraints, to roam and roar among us? Somehow I knew these things, somehow I could see the flinching muscles of his forelegs and flexing of his shoulders and fixing of his body as if to bound forward. And then he looked at me, not towards me, or in my direction, but directly into my eyes. He moved his head and looked straight at me. I felt rooted to the spot with both terror and bewilderment. How was this happening? What was he going to do? Was he going to attack me? My heart thumped in my chest so strongly my whole body shook. I felt my knees go wobbly and a stream of sweat run down my back under my shirt. We stood staring at each other for what felt like minutes but was probably only seconds. For both of us, for that period of time, nothing and no one else existed. His eyes looking into my eyes, both of us trying to read the other, were the only things that mattered at that time in the whole world. As I looked into his face, into his eyes, I started to lose my sense of terror and became more and more fascinated by what I was seeing. I began to feel a strong sense of familiarity, like I'd seen this before, like I'd dreamt it or something. And although still scared, it was more the sort of scared you feel riding a roller-coaster- thrilling rather than terrifying. And then the lion roared. He shook his mane, raised his head as if in a challenge, and roared so loudly it reverberated within my chest, like when you're in a club with a sound system with a super bass, that sort of vibration deep within the core of you. But the intensity of it was so strong that I felt my heart skip a beat or more, and start to pound erratically. I felt my breath catch, as if I thrown into a pool of ice-cold water, that sort of sharp shock. I knew I felt unwell, then. And that the lion was causing it. I didn't think he meant to but the power I was witnessing and the strength of his voice within me literally bowled me over, like I was seeing God or something. I felt myself groan, as if in response to him roar, a low moan came from my throat. And my head swam and I felt the world go topsy-turvy. And then the world rushed in. I could hear someone calling my name, as if from very far away. And then the collapse, down, hard, onto the ground, it's very real physicality bringing me back to myself with a shock, coming down to earth with a bump, you might say. And then I was aware of shoes, boys' and girls' shoes, and men's and women's, lots of them, around me. I remember noticing how scuffed one pair was and thinking that someone had breached the school rules by wearing trainers.

The rest is all a bit of a blur. There was a lot of commotion, a lot of people saying my name, my Uncle Edward's voice, commanding and authoritative, telling people to move away, to let him through, that he was a doctor. Then his voice calling my name, asking me if I could hear him? I remember thinking of course I could and making a response but he seemed not to hear, as if I hadn't spoken and maybe I hadn't, just thought I had. And then I remember being rolled over, onto my side, and the smell of aftershave familiar to me, and the sense of warmth and comfort and something placed over me, like a blanket but not really one, probably a coat. And something else placed under my head, to raise it from the cold ground. Someone's scarf, probably, a woman's I think as I smelt some perfume, strong, flowery and slightly sickly, like something an old woman would wear, too much. I remember the nausea rising in me, the sense of my mouth filling with saliva, knowing I was going to throw up, retching, but nothing in my stomach, just acid, a bitter, acrid taste in my mouth, again, different from before. Sounds from people gathered around me, sounds of disgust, moving their shoes away from me as I threw up. Teach them for standing around rubbernecking, I thought. Uncle Edward's voice again, more demanding this time, as he ordered people to stand back and to call an ambulance. Time passed and I remember being aware of more things around me, more clearly: the paramedics asking me my name, and how I was feeling and what had happened, and the sound of my own voice returning, answering their questions, as best as I could.

And then the lifting up onto the stretcher thing they use, being tucked in with a red blanket around me, being strapped in, the paramedic joking that they didn't want me bouncing around in the back, and then being hoisted up into the ambulance and seeing the Maiwand Lion, looking into the distance, motionless, as if nothing had happened.

CHAPTER TWO

The Royal Berkshire Hospital

The next time I felt like myself I was lying on a trolley in A+E in the Royal Berkshire Hospital. I remember looking up at the ceiling tiles, of being aware of hospital smells and sounds, and realising that something serious must have taken place if I'd ended up here. I also remember feeling incredibly tired, like I hadn't slept for days, or weeks even. But mainly I felt like I'd done something wrong, like I was in trouble. I must have drifted in and out for a time lying there, god knows how long but at some point I became aware of a light in my eyes, of someone lifting up my eyelid and focussing a light on my eyes. I was irritated by this and tried to shrug it away. Then something was causing pressure around my arm, and there was a hissing noise. I became aware gradually of the nurse, in her uniform, a sort of Virgin Mary blue, and her red hair tucked up, held in place by some clips and her freckles on her nose and her green eyes, smiling at me, like an angel. Angela O'Rourke, A+E nurse, Royal Berkshire Hospital NHS Trust, her name badge read. Even the photo on her ID badge looked concerned. Maybe I was going to be OK now, here, being looked after, by this nice lady, maybe as old as Mum, looking at me kindly with eyes full of concern and confidence and a quiet soft voice like someone on the radio, and an accent, Irish, like Gran's but a little bit softer, like that woman from the *Marks & Spencer's* ads on the TV:

'You're coming back to us now, Andrew, are you?' she smiled. 'You gave everyone a bit of a fright with all that carry on earlier but you seem to be fine now. How do you feel? Any headache?'

'No, thanks, I'm fine.' My voice sounded scratchy like I do when I have just woken up in the morning and I'm answering some question from

Mum about whether I want porridge or cereal, which she asks me every morning even though she knows I don't like her porridge because it's full of lumps and she can't get it right no matter how many times she tries to and she will never be like Gran who can make porridge as smooth as silk.

'Do you remember what happened before you became unwell, Andrew?' She talked to me like we'd known each other a lot longer than we did and used my name a lot.

'Not really,' I lied. I thought that if I said anything about what I'd really seen then they'd be getting me sectioned and locked up in Prospect Park with the other loons.

'Have you ever had episodes like this before, Andrew?' the nurse asked gently. I shook my head in response, deciding then that the less I said the less trouble I'd get myself into. I wasn't even sure if anything had really happened to me and felt a little guilty, like I was wasting people's time and making a fuss when there was nothing really wrong with me anyway. The nurse wrote some figures down on a chart on a clipboard thing and then said something about getting the doctor to 'give me the once over'. I asked her if Mum was around, or Uncle Edward.

'I think they're in the waiting area, Andrew. I'll go and let them know you're asking for them. They'll be pleased to know that you're feeling better.' She smiled her beatific smile and swished over the curtains around my cubicle with a practised movement, peeking around them one last time before closing then over again, like some dramatic little actress in a play.

And so I was alone, lying there, trying to figure out what the hell had happened to me. I had a feeling I was in trouble, for messing up the ceremony, that somehow I had brought the whole thing on myself. Obviously, I couldn't say anything about what I'd seen or they'd think I was going mad. Maybe I was, though. I replayed the scene over in my head again and thought how different these memories felt compared to remembering what I'd watched on TV last night, for example. They had a clarity and a confusion about them all at once.

Some doctor appeared then, more questions, asking whether I'd experienced any sort of 'aura' before the 'event' or if I'd ever had fits before or felt sometimes like I was 'out of myself ?' I laughed a little because it seemed funny to me: 'What, like an out-of-body experience or something?' He smiled weakly back and explained that sometimes people with certain types of epilepsy feel as if they are 'dissociated' from the world around them before they have a seizure. I denied feeling anything like that, just said I'd probably not eaten breakfast that morning because my mother makes lumpy porridge and we'd run out of cereal. I laughed a little, like I was making light of it, and he smiled too, a little, like he understood but wasn't convinced. He asked me some stupid questions, like did I know who the Prime Minister was (of course I bloody did because he was that fool Gordon Brown who kept us in Afghanistan even though he'd let us believe that when he took over from Tony Blair that he'd take us out of the war), and some mental arithmetic (which I could do better than him), and then he started to get me to do things with my face, to test my cranial nerves (I knew this from Uncle Edward telling me about it before) and then he looked into my eyes with an ophthalmoscope which was attached to the wall with a cord that looked like one of those old-fashioned phones you see on movies from the '70s. I could smell his aftershave and a faint smell of garlic on his breath even though he tried not to breathe when examining me. Then he checked my arms and legs, pulling, pushing, pointing and pricking me with things to see if I had any 'sensory or motor deficit'.

By the time he'd finished with me I'd felt a bit warmer towards him and realised he was trying to help me. But my hostility initially was due to a fear that he might unearth what I was keeping to myself and also that he might expose me as a time-waster and a fraud. I knew that I didn't have a seizure or anything like that, even if I didn't really understand what else could explain what I'd seen and felt this morning. I just knew nothing was wrong with me, not physically anyway. And I started to feel a bit sorry for this doctor, about ten years older than me and obviously busy but doing his best to help me. By the end of his examination, he smiled at me and told me that everything seemed to be as it should be but that they'd want to keep me in for at least 24 hours for observation and to do more tests. I reacted badly to being told that I'd be in hospital overnight, mainly because I worried that this would add to the amount of trouble I'd eventually be in with everyone if I wasted the time of NHS doctors and nurses as well as missing school and messing up the ceremony. I protested that I'd prefer to go home now, please. But he said that it would be better for everyone, including my parents, if I stayed in a bit longer to allow everyone to be certain I was okay.

'I don't have parents,' I corrected him. 'At least, I don't have a father anymore. He was killed a few months ago, in Afghanistan...' I felt my voice catch again. It seemed every time I mentioned anything about my Dad that my voice cracked, like my voice was strangled when trying to speak his name. The doctor seemed to notice this, too, and said, softly: 'I'm sorry, Andrew. I didn't know about that. I'm sorry for your loss. That must be very hard for you, and your family. How are you all coping, if I may ask?'

I shrugged my shoulders, trying to appear nonchalant. I'd gotten practiced at this, concerned not to let people get too upset by talking to me about my Dad, about 'my loss'. 'Y'know, it's been tough. But we're coping- no choice, really.'

'Sure,' said the doctor, gently. 'It's never easy to lose anyone, especially your parents. Were you very close?'

And then my eyes started to fill up, again! I felt my chin wobble and my voice, when I tried to speak, sounded so strangled, even I couldn't understand what I was trying to say. And then I felt the doctor touch my hand, then grip it, to squeeze it reassuringly, and touched my shoulder with his other hand, to comfort me, I guess. I felt a little embarrassed but mainly better for his concern. He spoke softer still then:

'Sounds like you've had quite a time of it, Andrew. Lots on your plate. I'm sure it's hard on you, dealing with all this. Do you have brothers or sisters?' I shook my head.

'So you're dealing with all this on your own, then? Trying to be brave in front of your Mum? There's no shame in asking for help, y'know. Everyone copes in different ways. And sometimes if we keep things bottled up, well, they come out in different ways.' I could see where he was going with this, thinking I was some traumatised kid not dealing with his grief and having some episode as a result. I knew about 'psychosomatic illnesses' and how people with all sorts of psychiatric problems could present with weird illnesses, funny turns, skin rashes, paralysis and stuff. We'd learned a bit about it doing history, when we studied the First World War and learned about soldiers from the front ending up in hospitals with hysterical blindness or not being able to walk or feel things. They called it shell shock but we now know it was a sort of post-traumatic stress disorder. They couldn't face the horror of what they were seeing and having to deal with so their minds took them out of action. And maybe that was what was happening to me? Maybe, I wasn't half as well as I thought I was. I had been mainly embarrassed by the loss of my Dad, or at least in dealing with it in public, when people were expressing their sympathies, like it was something that wasn't polite to talk about and a bit cringe-worthy when people tried to talk to me about it. I remember the day his body was repatriated. We all travelled, as a family, to Wotton Basset, in Wiltshire, where the airbase was located where his body, his 'remains', would be flown 'home'. The people there had become rather famous now in the country with their observance of the return of the dead. There had never been such a thing in the history of warfare in this country, people lining the streets and paying their respects to the fallen 'heroes' returning from the front. Usually, soldiers were buried where they died. But no one could contemplate the horror of leaving the remains of loved ones in that parched damned blood-soaked earth, lying there at the mercy of the Taliban, at risk of having their graves defiled. And as there was nothing ordinary people could do about anything so big as a war, they did what people often do and did something small but kind to show they felt the pain of the bereaved, the maimed and the dead. They lined the streets, cried together with us, threw flowers onto the hearses as they passed, and even applauded quietly and respectfully, to show that they understood there was a human being passing by who had done something amazing, had given up their life for their country. But did their country ask them for such a sacrifice? Or did anyone ask our opinion? Did they listen to the million strong protest march in London the February before the March the war began in Iraq? Did the US Presidents or UK Prime Ministers have children or brothers or fathers or daughters or mothers or sisters 'in theatre'? Would they have to stand there on an overcast day in August among the crowd when their own father passed them by in a hearse? Or feel the eyes of the crowd on them as their mother gently pushed them forward to place flowers on the hearse's roof when it paused before us, the chief mourners, the other families bereaved that time standing huddled together with mine. There were three coffins that day, draped in the Union Jack, and three sets of families coping in their own way with the hole left in their lives by the death of these men, doing their jobs, and murdered by the Taliban and for a cause no one bar the government seemed to understand. I had not thought about that moment since it had happened. The thoughts now seemed to be bubbling up unbidden. They brought hot tears to my eyes, grief, yes but anger and confusion, too. I thought I had moved on from these feelings but perhaps I'd simply trained myself not to think about them, had 'repressed' them. And then the Maiwand Lion roared and broke through my defences and left me here, crying, on a trolley in the A+E Department in a hospital in Reading, a mile away from the War Memorial and a lifetime away from my father.

Uncle Edward may have been there for a few moments before I came to realise it. The junior doctor smiled at him, said something about leaving us to talk together and nodded, respectfully, at Uncle Edward, and left. I turned my head over to meet his gaze, full of concern but not entirely unclinical, as he scanned me for signs of any disorder or disease, his brain no doubt flicking through an entire list of differential diagnoses. He often told me that the job of a good doctor was to look mostly, listen acutely and speak sparingly if he was to make a diagnosis properly, or allow the diagnosis to reveal itself. He said that when he'd trained in America, they had relied mainly on various clinical tests and laboratory investigations to make diagnoses that were often more easily elicited if a person with the right skills took the time to study the patient and gently prod and probe the problem until it surfaced. This tradition went all the way back to Hippocrates, he said, and we lost it at our peril because no matter what modern science tried to tell us, humans were more than the sum of their biochemical and neurological processes. But now I felt that probing intensely focussed on me, I thought how preferable it would be to have only to undergo whatever scans or tests the young doctor was lining up for me. I was sure they could not see into me, the way Uncle Edward could. And because I was feeling mainly that I had caused the problem myself, somehow, and that it was the work of a mind still coming to terms with lots of big issues, I did not want him in my head, at least not until I'd figured out what was going on in there myself. I knew he was only concerned for my well-being and did not suspect him of wishing to see me get into trouble. It then occurred to me that if I could convince him that there was nothing really wrong with me, then perhaps I could make this whole episode go away, and become one of those slightly embarrassing family stories that never get spoken about again but which everyone knows lurk under the surface of all their interactions from that point forward.

'How are you feeling, Andrew?' he asked, concern in his voice but trying to sound upbeat, too. He approached me and looked into my eyes, while rubbing my hair, like he used to when I was younger. 'Your Mum was terribly upset when you had your 'little turn' earlier but I've said to her that most likely it was just something like a dip in your blood sugar, coupled with all the obvious emotion of the day.' He sounded awkward talking to me, unusual for him, normally so eloquent and in control. I could see he was trying to convince himself as much as anyone else that what was going on with me was nothing to be concerned about.

'Yeah, I'm feeling fine, now, just very tired. The doctor doesn't really know what has happened but he wants to keep me in for observation and some tests.'

'Oh?' Uncle Edward raised one eyebrow in an expression almost caricaturist in its appearance. He was letting me tell my story, like the good doctor he was, just luring me in with an expression of interest.

'Yeah, well, he said it was probably just something minor or something but he wants to check me out for things like epilepsy and stuff like that. I suppose that will mean me being wired up to some machine to read my 'brainwaves' or something?'

'An EEG, yes, probably.'

'And a CT scan or something, he said. But do you think I need to have all this done? I mean, it is probably something trivial, not worth wasting everyone's time over, don't you think?'

Uncle Edward smiled and said that the whole reason doctors and nurses worked in hospitals was to do this sort of work and that it was better to have the tests done and be reassured that nothing serious had happened that to ignore a potentially serious problem, not that he thought that's what they'd find with me.

'You have been through quite a bit, lately,' he smiled gently. 'I'm sure it all takes its toll in ways which none of us expected. And I know that you'll be fine and that we'll all be fine. We'll get through it together, won't we? We don't want to cause your mother any unnecessary concern, do we? So I suggest we just let all these good people get on with their jobs and get you sorted out as soon as possible. And if that means staying a night or two then so what? I'm sure you'll catch up with the little bit of school work quite quickly, a bright chap like you. And it will help the whole family to know that you're fit and healthy.'

I knew then that Uncle Edward was telling me what I needed to do in order to reassure everyone. And I knew then that he was not going to be any sort of ally in avoiding the hospital admission. And perhaps most of all, I knew he also knew damned well that there was nothing wrong with me, at least not physically, and that he knew I was withholding something from him. But like the good doctor he was, he would stick to the process of eliminating any possible risk of physical causes before taking action on what was left, psychiatric illness.

CHAPTER THREE

Medusa

'Do you want porridge or cereal for breakfast, Andrew?' was the first thing I remember my mother asking me that morning before we went to see the shrink, about two weeks after the doctors at the Royal Berks had confirmed that they could not find any 'organic' cause for my 'event' but felt, given the circumstances of my recent 'bereavement' then it would be useful for me to meet with a counsellor. I remember Mum still being in her dressing gown standing in our kitchen with a cup of coffee in her hand as she questioned me about my choice of breakfast. I raised my eyes to whatever deity exists and said I'd just have some *Kellogg's Crunchy Nut Cornflakes*, like I do every morning.

'Are you sure you wouldn't prefer something hot? It's really cold this morning.' She pulled her dressing gown closer to her body as she said this as if to demonstrate the veracity of her comment on the weather in late November. I shook my head and proceeded to pour myself a bowl of cereal, even though I would have preferred porridge with some honey, if Gran had made it.

'Look at the time!' she exclaimed a bit dramatically. 'I'd better get into the shower. There's some coffee left in the pot if you want some, but not too much, you don't want to get over-stimulated before your session.'

'Session' was a word she'd picked up from some TV show to try to make the fact I was seeing a shrink a bit less wacked than it really was, like it was just another 'lifestyle choice'. I knew Gran thought it was all a waste of time and that I'd be better off just dealing with things whatever way I found easiest myself. But unfortunately Uncle Edward agreed that it would be helpful to get some 'space to talk through the experiences I'd had with a professional, someone outside of the family.' This was the closest he'd ever come to admitting that our family was wacked and that the only chance I'd ever have of sorting myself out was to get outside help. I'd decided to play along with their little charade if for no other reason than to annoy my mother. She'd been really irritating me lately and that numpty of a 'friend' of hers, Jonathan, was around far too often for my liking. Maybe if he thought she had a kid that was cracking up then he'd think twice before getting more involved with her, with us. He was a solicitor with the firm she worked for as an administrator. I often wondered whether this was entirely kosher, whether he was allowed to mix it up with his staff. Mum denied there was anything between them other than friendship. 'I'm allowed friends, Andrew, just like you are, y'know!' she responded sharply when I'd challenged her about it before. I always shrugged and said 'whatever'. I couldn't believe his motives would be so pure, irrespective of what she thought about their 'friendship'. When she scrubbed up and made the effort, Mum was a reasonably good looking woman, for someone her age. She had a good figure, her face wasn't too wrinkled and her hair was a sort of strawberry blonde, which hid most of the grey. She dressed well, too: not mumsy but not slaggy either. She got her clothes for work from *M&S* but bought the odd special thing from *John Lewis*. She'd been shopping there a lot lately, buying new tops and things. I knew she was shopping for him, her friend. He was taking her out to plays in London and for dinner in *The Forbury* restaurant and stuff. So she didn't want him to see her in the same outfit all the time.

'Why would that matter if you were just friends?' I'd asked her before. 'I don't care if Ash or Natasha turn up in the same thing every time we go to the cinema, do I?'

The news was on the radio. I listened to it as I was munching through my cornflakes. The newscaster said that two more British soldiers had been killed by roadside bombs in Sangin province in Afghanistan, the

Ministry of Defence had announced today. Their identities would not be revealed until their families had been informed. I stopped eating for a moment and thought about how some kid somewhere today might be about to learn that his father, or mother, had been killed. This made me feel sad but mainly angry. It seemed that nothing was changing. Some politician came on the radio then saying how the government recognised the high price being paid by British service men and women and their families but that this 'operation' was essential for British security and that all efforts would be made to limit both British and Afghan casualties. The guy interviewing the politician then asked about some incident where Afghan civilians had been killed in a rocket attack on a village by the Americans. The politician gave some line about how all civilian deaths were regrettable but that the Taliban were using innocent civilians as cover for their operations and that it was in the interest of both NATO forces and the Afghan people themselves to see them defeated. The interviewer didn't seem that convinced by the politician's answer but it was time for the sports' report so he thanked him for his time and moved on to let us know about how Manchester United had done in some match yesterday.

Mum drove me to the place where the counsellor worked. It was one of those old Victorian buildings which used to be someone's home once but was now divided up into offices. The waiting room was once someone's 'drawing room' probably. There was one other woman sitting there when we went in. My mother smiled at her when we entered but she just turned away and kept her eyes focussed on the *Hello* magazine she was reading. I looked at Mum and mouthed 'loon' to her and she laughed a little, despite ticking me off for making the comment. The receptionist was a nice plump Asian woman in a blue suit who took our details and told us that 'Helena' was running slightly behind at the present time but would get to us as soon as possible and to take a seat. We sat down on a sort of leather couch thing.

'You don't have to wait here, Mum. I've told you I'm happy to see the shrink by myself. I am fifteen after all.' Mum was trying to find a

28

magazine less than two years old from the dog-eared pile on the coffee table before us. 'No, I told you she wants to see us both, as a family, to see how we get on and...' She stumbled with trying to phrase the next comment appropriately so I jumped in instead.

'And how we're coping with our "loss".' I made that gesture with my fingers wiggling in the air which I'd seen people on TV shows do to indicate they were being ironic by using words they didn't agree with. Mum just looked impatiently at me and tight-lipped and told me to 'drop the attitude'.

The woman who'd been sitting in the waiting room when we'd come in was then called by the receptionist and went through to another room. 'God, we'll be here forever if we've to wait for her to be sorted out!' I hissed. My Mum hushed me but I could see that she thought what I'd said was funny. I huffed and sat back into the couch, crossing my arms in a determined show of boredom. I looked out the window as I spoke, avoiding Mum's gaze.

'This is a complete waste of time, y'know,' I complained. 'What's this woman going to tell me, anyway? They don't know what caused my problem in the Royal Berks, and they're proper doctors. What's this head shrink going to do to help? Tell me I'm upset about losing my Dad and that's what caused me to collapse in front of the whole town at the Remembrance Sunday ceremony?'

'She's just going to try to get to know us, Andrew.' Mum used that sort of patient voice she uses when she's trying to avoid sounding irritated when explaining something very obvious to someone who just doesn't get it. She used to use it a lot with Dad, when they were together. He didn't like it, either.

'Why is she "trying to get to know us"?' I did the finger wiggle in the air thing again. 'What does she care about us? It's just a job to her. This interest she has in us wouldn't exist if someone didn't pay her, would it?'

'Look, Andrew'. Mum's patience was clearly wearing thin. 'We have been sent here to get some support for you and to try to help us both (she hesitated, again) come to terms with what's happened to us as a family, and to try to move forward together.'

'Seems to me that you've moved on already. Nice time with Jonathan, last night?' Mum grabbed my arm and forced me to look her in the face. She glared at me with something more like anger than annoyance.

'Will you stop doing that, please? I've told you before about this. I have nothing to apologise for in having friends or in doing things with them that I enjoy. And you have no right to make me feel bad about it, either. If this is about making me feel guilty, Andrew, then it's not going to work. I have every right to expect your support for me in making friends and getting on with my life, just like you have every right to expect my support.' I shrugged her arm off, turning my head away again.

'Yes, it's all about you, Mum, isn't it?'

She softened her tone then, through an act of self-control I knew she was finding hard. 'Look, Andrew. This isn't how we should be together. You know I love you and I have no interest in doing anything that would hurt you. I'm here with you to show you that I'm concerned about you and want to get you the help that you need.'

'And what help is that, Mum? What can anyone say to me to make up for the fact that Dad is dead? That he was murdered by a bunch of savages thousands of miles away? That they took him away from me and that there is nothing I can do about it? How can someone make that go away? They can't. This is a complete waste of time. I don't know why I even agreed to do this. Completely stupid.'

A thought formed in my head that I would just get up and walk out the door and leave Mum sitting there to talk to the stupid therapist by herself, so that it could be about her again. She'd probably enjoy that anyway. But the receptionist suddenly spoke, politely but firmly, pulling me back to where I was.

'Is everything OK, please? Do you have a problem I can help with?' Mum seemed suddenly embarrassed, realising that our little spat had been overheard.

'Sorry, no. Thank you,' she stumbled, touching my forearm, indicating that I should sit down, sit back, stay calm.

'It's always difficult, these sort of things,' the receptionist continued, smiling. 'Boys and their mothers. I should know, I have four sons.'

'Really?' Mum replied. I knew she was just being polite but she was also irritated by the intrusion of this random stranger into her affairs.

'Well, you know, I also have three daughters. A great help they are to me, too. But there is something special about the bond between a mother and her sons. They need us yet their pride is hurt by knowing this.' She chuckled to herself at this little gem of wisdom. 'You have a fine looking son, my dear. And you, young man, have a beautiful mother. Such a lovely face and beautiful hair. I can see where you get your good looks from!' She giggled girlishly, and made me feel a bit embarrassed, talking about me like that and all. But somehow it seemed to diffuse the situation and we all laughed a little, Mum looking at me and smiling.

'Yes, my son is very handsome, I agree. But he's even lovelier when you get to know him.' I blushed at this display of maternal affection.

'You are making him blush! Look at how red he goes! Oh, he'll break some hearts when he's older, I bet. Look what a wonderful smile he has!' she gently ribbed me and made me laugh. We all laughed a little together. And somehow the tension had gone.

The door opened and the grumpy woman who'd been in with the therapist walked back into the waiting room, somewhat surprised by the obvious mirth which was in play.

It wasn't long before we were entering into the therapist's office. A plump woman, with a mass of wavy grey hair only slightly brought under control by a sort of large butterfly clip thing clamped to the back of her head, sat on a battered leather armchair, sipping on a coffee cup, and, on noticing our arrival, hastily dropped the cup into a saucer on a little side-table beside the chair, clattering the china noisily, and beckoned us to sit down on a large padded chintz covered sofa which had definitely seen better days. She smiled in introduction, causing the faint black moustache over her lip to spread. Her dark green cardigan seemed to have been hand-knitted and the equally green blouse underneath had several coffee stains down the front of her ample breasts. She wore a large silver fob thing on a neck chain which I later realised was actually a watch, which she wound absent-mindedly several times during the 'session'. Her tweed brown skirt covered tree trunk-like legs over which prominent varicose veins wriggled under her thick tan tights. On her feet she wore some sort of moccasin things, one of which she dangled from her toes, as she crossed her legs and slumped back into her armchair. It was only later that I realised these were actually slippers as I spotted a sturdy pair of outdoor shoes parked under a desk against the far wall.

'I'm Helena,' she said, 'and I presume you are Mrs. Connolly and this must be Andrew?'

Mum shook the woman's offered hand politely but I just sort of nodded at her when she said my name. 'Well, it's really lovely to meet you both. I always think it is helpful for us to tell each other a little about ourselves when I meet new patients and get some idea about what we expect to get out of our time together. Does that sound OK to you both?' Before we could do anything other than exchange quizzical glances with each other, the woman launched into a speech she had obviously said many times before.

'I'm Doctor Helena Markiewicz and I've been working as a psychiatrist for, well, let's just say before Andrew was born and leave it as that, shall we?' She smiled conspiratorially at Mum who smiled weakly back. 'I am here to see if I can help you and Andrew to understand what is happening to you both and to see if we can work together to help you both move forward towards a happier and healthier place. I expect that we will be frank and honest with each other and that we will work together. I am not here to 'fix' anyone and I do not think that is even possible, actually. I am not here to trick anyone or to send anyone to an institution of any kind. And I am not here to fill anyone full of psychotropic drugs, unless it is absolutely necessary to do so. Now, that's why I'm here and that's what I expect, so let's hear from you two, now. Mrs. Connolly, do you mind if I call you Kathryn, good, much better to drop the formalities, I think, and you can call me Helena, both of you, do you want to start and tell us why you are here and what you expect from this work?'

Mum shuffled forward on the sofa, her handbag clasped protectively in front of her against the Medusa stare of the batty psychiatrist who waited expectantly for her to speak.

'Well,' she hesitated, 'I am Kathryn Connolly, as you know (she smiled weakly as if to apologise for her gaucheness) and I'm Andrew's mother. I guess I am here today to help my son, who has been dealing with some very difficult things since the death of his father in the summer and...' Suddenly, her voice caught and her eyes teared up.

'My dear, don't upset yourself. Here, dry your eyes,' said Dr. Markiewicz, passing her a box of tissues which appeared in a practiced manner from the side of the armchair.

'Sorry, I don't know why I'm behaving like this,' Mum said as she dabbed her eyes and her nose, then looking at me said: 'Sorry, Andrew. I didn't mean to embarrass you with all this sort of carry on, I know it upsets you.'

'Well, Andrew. Why don't we give your Mum a moment or two to compose herself and ask you to say a little about yourself and what you expect from this work we are about to undertake?'

I shrugged and looked away from the intense gaze of the shrink. I felt a bit stupid introducing myself so I said something about her knowing all about me from the letters the doctors at the RBH had already sent to her, no doubt and that I was here because they thought I was losing it because my Dad had been killed and I was having some sort of grief reaction or something which had caused me to collapse at the Remembrance Day ceremony.

'Well, yes, Andrew,' she said slowly, speaking like a patient teacher to a stupid kid, 'your doctors did write to me, as I'm sure they told you, and yes, I do know about the event you experienced at the Remembrance Sunday ceremony but that's not what I asked you. I asked you to tell me something about yourself and what you expected from the work we are going to do together over the next few weeks or whatever. Could you do that for me, please? I promise I won't bite.' She smiled a smile which suddenly transformed her face from a scrutinizing shrink to a kindly aunt enquiring after her favourite nephew. I suppose that relaxed me a bit and so I said that I was Andrew Connolly, aged fifteen, a student at St. Edward the Martyr's Catholic School, doing my GCSEs this year. I lived with my Mum, in Caversham. We had lived together, alone, in Reading since moving here when I was twelve so that I could go to a good school. We had family here, Uncle Edward and Gran, who lived nearby.

'And what about your Dad, Andrew. Did he move to Reading with you when you came here three years ago?'

I looked at Mum, maybe seeking her permission to talk about something which was personal to her as well as to me with this woman we hardly knew. Mum nodded encouragingly, dabbing her nose still with the tissues the shrink had given her.

'No, my Dad didn't come here with us. Mum and Dad split up around then and he stayed with the Army when we came here. He did visit us, me, though. At least, at first. He was posted to Iraq twice and then went to Afghanistan, his first time actually, which is where he was killed...' I trailed off because my voice caught. I kept doing that which was really irritating me because it left the impression that I wasn't coping with Dad's death but I was, I really was. It was just that when I talked about him it seemed to trigger something in my throat so it became tight and my spit dried up or something. As usual, the batty shrink pounced on this apparent show of emotion.

'Go on, Andrew. I know it's difficult to talk about these things but it's what we're here to do, you know and if I do all the talking then how would that look, eh? You'd be asking for your money back, wouldn't you?' She chuckled in an effort to cajole me into opening up and, despite myself, I found the old bat a bit more OK, like she was one of Gran's friends, slightly mad in that old person sort of way but nice and interested in you and the things you say and do. Probably because there is so little going on in their own lives apart for waiting for God, as Dad used to say. He didn't like Gran so much, said she was always interfering in things between him and Mum, even when we didn't live in the same town as her. That's one of the reasons he didn't come here with us, because Gran would be nearby. Or maybe that's why Mum chose Reading, so that she would be surrounded by people who Dad didn't like, like Gran and Uncle Edward. He never did like Uncle Edward much either, now that I think about it. But he made more of an effort with him than with Gran, perhaps because Mum and Uncle Edward were so close or maybe because he knew I wanted to be a doctor like Uncle Edward and he didn't want to get on the wrong side of him, like that could do my career some harm as Uncle Edward was an important consultant in Oxford so he would probably be the wrong person to have against you if you were trying to get into the medical world around here. That was Dad, always thinking two steps ahead and looking after me, my interests. He told me that, too. That he'd always be there for me. He told me that everyone needs someone in their life they can turn to, no matter what, no matter how terrible things are or even terrible things they've done, and that was what he meant to be to me, the one I could always turn to. But he was gone now, so I suppose he didn't really keep his promise, after all. And maybe that's why I didn't just feel sad or lonely now that he was gone but I also felt angry, really angry at times.

Because he put himself in harm's way and now he was gone and I had to go on knowing that there was never going to be anyone else who would always be there for me, whatever.

'What about school, then, Andrew?' asked the shrink, perhaps sensing that shifting gear to a more neutral subject was the better course of action at this time. 'Do you enjoy it?'

'It's alright, I guess,' I shrugged.

Mum suddenly piped up, saying I was a great student, that all my teachers said so, and that they were expecting great things from me, good GCSEs, then Sixth Form College and university, maybe to study medicine. Her voice sounded strong and confident as she said these things. But mainly proud, even boastful.

'Well, quite a scholar then, Andrew, by the sounds of things?' Dr. Markiewicz winked. 'But do you enjoy it? Any friends?'

'Yeah, y'know. A few good friends, Ash and Natasha, mainly. But the school's alright and teachers are OK, I s'ppose.'

'And what about subjects, do you have any favourite subjects?'

'Yeah, I like science, biology especially. I need to do this well to be a doctor. And Uncle Edward talks to me about stuff he's working on and cases and stuff so that's interesting.'

'Uncle Edward? Is that your Mum's brother, then?'

I nodded in answer. 'He's at consultant at the Churchill Hospital in Oxford'.

'Very impressive,' Dr. Markiewicz beamed sounding over-impressed in some fake way which irked me. Probably jealous because Uncle Edward was a real doctor and not some shrink, like her. Uncle Edward always said that shrinks might have studied medicine at some stage in their career but two years into their rotation they forgot which end of a stethoscope to use and spent their whole life trying to convince everyone that all the patients they saw had anything other than a psychiatric illness going on. They 'turfed' people to the care of any other type of specialist, from infectious diseases to dermatology, just to get rid of them, or at least delay having to deal with them. That's why I was surprised that this old shrink had taken me on so readily but I suppose that she was assessing me with a view to batting me back to my GP. Or maybe, the fact that we were paying privately to see her, or at least Uncle Edward was, made her more accepting of her patient.

'And have you talked to your Uncle about your recent experiences, Andrew?' the shrink asked, probably trying to see if he had figured out what was going on in my head and save her the trouble of having to do so.

'Yeah, a bit,' I shrugged. 'He said that all my tests had been normal and that there was no sign of any epilepsy or brain lesions to explain my symptoms....'

She chuckled as I answered. 'I don't mean did you have a 'case conference', Andrew. I meant if you had talked about all of the recent events in your life, about your Dad, and how that makes you feel?'

I shrugged again, saying yeah, of course we talked about stuff but we didn't really dwell on all the negative things. That Uncle Edward had been brilliant, a great support to me and Mum and Gran after Dad had died. That I couldn't ask for a better uncle. But the thing he helped me with most was getting back to normal, telling me that it was important to try to get on with my life, get on with school and studying. To try to keep my life on track, because that's what my Dad would have wanted for me. Then my bloody voice cracked again, really irritated me because it gave Medusa the chance to pounce again.

'And do you think you were ready to get on with things, Andrew?'

'Yeah, well, y'know, it was hard at first. Especially meeting all my friends when we went back to school in September. Everyone was a bit awkward and stuff, even the teachers. People said nice things, though. Everyone was kind and the teachers told me that if I needed to take time out or needed any extra help with things that I should talk to them and stuff.' My voice trailed off again. I realised how saying this stuff out loud made me realise that for much of the last few months I had been more interested in appearing 'normal' to everyone so that they didn't feel awkward around me, 'cos they did, especially at first. That first few days back at school were really weird. It all felt a bit unreal, like I was watching a movie or something. Like there was a glass wall between me and everyone else. And all the stupid little things we use to squabble about or fret about or get worked up about all seemed a bit stupid now and unimportant. And it seemed that some of the other people I use to mix with a lot sort of peeled away from me, or at least that's what I felt. Except for Ash, who was just as annoying and irritating as always, banging on about Doctor Who trivia, as if it mattered. And maybe Natasha, although she wasn't really normal with me, sort of changed in a way in her behaviour towards me, appearing a bit more concerned about me. I thought at first she might be interested in me, y'know, not just as friends. But then I realised that she was just being kind, that I was one of her 'causes' now, like saving the planet and the rain forest and reducing carbon footprints and shit like that, as if any of it really mattered, as if we could save a planet, as if it was even worth saving, as if people wouldn't kill each other one way or the other over something or other, oil or land or religion or sex or whatever.

'That must have been nice for you, Andrew, having such supportive friends and teachers? I bet they all rallied around and helped, didn't they?'

I sort of nodded in agreement.

'But do you think they really got what was happening to you?' she continued, staring into my eyes with her cold blue eyes. 'Do you think they even got a fraction of the enormity of the thing that was happening to you? That your world had turned upside down and inside out in a way none of them could really understand? Do you think they could even fathom the depth of anger you felt toward the people who killed your father, or perhaps even the anger you felt towards everyone who hadn't suffered as you had, who perhaps made some stupid trite statement to you about how sorry they were for your loss, perhaps even saying something about how brave your father was, about how important the war was for Britain, when all you wanted to do was either crawl up into a ball and never come out, or smash their stupid faces into a bloody pulp?' She shook her own fist in the air before us and then thumped the arm of her chair, causing my Mum to jump slightly, so unexpected was the action, so vehement the emotion from this bag-lady of a shrink, so intent was her stare, as if she was reading my soul through my eyes. I could feel her in my head, like she had a thousand little tentacles crawling all over my cortex.

The moment hung there for a second or two before anyone spoke. She held my stare, reading the slightly astonished expression on my face, seeing the impact of her words etched there, enjoying her little triumph too, no doubt. She resumed suddenly, so matter-of-factly.

'All perfectly normal feelings, Andrew, I can assure you. And all perfectly healthy, too. No one can really understand something like what you've been through unless it's happened to them, can they? No one can appreciate the feelings you're having, can they? And that makes you feel alone, apart, separate, doesn't it? And no one can help you feel better, not really, can they? Especially not some old baggage like me, eh?' She chuckled. I looked at my Mum, she was looking at the shrink, like she couldn't quite believe what she was hearing. She slowly turned her head towards me when she realised that I was staring at her. Our eyes met for a second. It felt as if she was seeing me completely differently for that moment. That she was suddenly realising something important. I looked away. I looked at my shoes. I cleared my throat.

'No. No one can understand me, what I'm going through. No one who hasn't had a father murdered, for something which no one understands, not really. I don't even understand what I'm supposed to feel. I just know I want this feeling to stop, and I don't know if it ever will.' I stopped speaking then and let the feeling wash over me, let the loneliness and the sadness manifest themselves in the room like another person. I felt a hand touch mine, warm, soft and something clicked inside me and I felt somehow a bit better. I touched my mother's hand with mine and held it there a second or two or more and we said nothing just touched and stayed quiet and let the thing remain unsaid.

CHAPTER FOUR

Revelation

Ash was showing me some new website, typing focussedly, tapping away on my laptop while I half-looked, some blog about *Doctor Who* and the new actor playing him and his new assistant, a 'flame-haired Scottish beauty, with a quick quip and a quirky sense of fashion' according to the blogger 'breaking the news' to Whovians the world over, of which Ash was undoubtedly the nerdiest of the nerds. He could hardly contain his excitement about some of the spoilers coming through from the worldwide network of dweebs who cared about this sort of shit. I suppose if the world was as crap as it was, then looking for something better in the imagination was the most logical response. Apparently the Tardis had been given a makeover, too. Ash wasn't too sure about this as, like most sci-fi nuts, he was an arch conservative and painfully loyal to storylines, with any continuity error or non sequitar in the script of a long-running TV series bugging him in a way that only other obsessive compulsives could fathom. His love of sci-fi and fantasy knew no bounds. He had a passing grasp of Elfish, Klingon and even a smattering of Vulcan. His only true regret in life was that *Starfleet Academy* didn't really exist as he would have enrolled as soon as it was possible. He was convinced that he had been born out of his true 'timeline' and that at some point this catastrophic error would be accounted for. Quantum mechanics allowed for the possibility of other universes, multi-verses, and in one of these he really was the science officer on-board a *Galaxy Class* starship.

His love of physics was driven by a sense of a future when, he believed, we would have cracked some of the great challenges of now, be it faster than light travel or efficient fusion engines or teleportation. He was the only person I knew who had a picture of Stephen Hawking as his screensaver and followed his hero's career the way most boys followed their favourite football team. When Hawking appeared on an episode of *Star Trek*, he got so excited he nearly wet himself, his head almost exploding in the collision of his real and fantasy worlds.

'The new series will have this ongoing storyline about cracks in the fabric of space and time,' he explained excitedly about the forthcoming *Doctor Who* shows, due to air that following Easter.

' *"A series of strange signs and portents lead to an unexpected twist placing the Doctor at the centre of a chain of causality where cause and effect become so entwined it is impossible to distinguish one from the other",'* he read aloud excitedly.

'Yeah, but do you really believe in all of that crap, though?' I asked provocatively. 'I mean the idea of time travel and stuff. Like, if it was really possible wouldn't we already have it? Wouldn't someone have gone back in time and killed Hitler? Or stopped those people crashing jumbo jets into the Twin Towers?'

Ash looked at my face, judging my tone, seeing if I was really just talking about theoretical physics or if I was asking something a lot more personal. He guessed that I wasn't really looking at it truly objectively.

'Well, I guess there would be rules or something, like the temporal prime directive they talk about in *Star Trek*, y'know? I presume only government agencies would be able to time travel, 'cos it would be so expensive to build a time machine. So maybe they would ensure that only authorised journeys were made, so that human history couldn't be changed.'

'What, not even for the better?' I challenged. 'What sort of government wouldn't think killing Hitler was a good idea? Or Stalin? Or Osama bin Laden? Who could object to killing bastards like that?'

'Well, there might be wider considerations,' Ash answered cautiously. 'You know, the stone in the pond effect, where even the smallest of changes ripples out and impacts upon lots of other things, some of which might be even more disastrous than anything we know about.'

'But what about all that stuff about "multiple realities" that you're always going on about, where decisions made one way or the other are all played out, so somewhere, in an alternate universe, the planes that flew into the Twin Towers were shot down before they reached their target, or where the bombers in London on 7/7 were intercepted before they got onto the Tube, or where my Dad became a plasterer instead of a soldier and still lived with Mum and me, here, in Reading?' I could feel my throat tightening at the mention of my Dad's name, feel my face reddening, and could see Ash looking increasingly awkward and uncomfortable. He looked at his shoes for a moment and shrugged his shoulders.

'Well, I guess it's complicated, that's why we haven't figured it out yet.'

I felt bad for making him feel bad, so I tried to lighten the mood.

'And in some other reality you're Casey Grant's boyfriend and she isn't going out with that Neanderthal Jimmy Jackson.' We both laughed, Ash blushed a bit and shrugged off the suggestion with 'Her loss!' and got back to the screen, typing away, now on *Facebook*. I saw Natasha's face appear on the screen, some new pictures of her at a 16th birthday party she'd attended, looking happy and pretty and all made-up and grown-up looking. I thought how both Ash and I looked so young in comparison, just boys really, awkward and unfashionable and nerdy and swotty. But I guess that was just how it was for us, and we didn't really care too much about girlfriends and stuff. And I thought that most boys in our class probably exaggerated about their conquests anyway. But it sort of bothered me that it was another way in which I'd failed my Dad. He wouldn't have been so backward at my age in such things. He'd already joined up at sixteen and was married to my Mum at 21. She was actually a bit older than him, at 23 when she'd married. I think she was pregnant with me at the time, although she's never come right out and said it, but I was born just six months later so it makes sense. Uncle

Edward disapproved of Dad, didn't think he was good enough for Mum, blamed him for her dropping out of university before completing her degree. They had been going out with each other for a couple of years by then and Mum said she'd simply realised that she didn't want to spend the best years of her life reading books about lives other people had lived but wanted to live her own life. But it still upset Uncle Edward, who thought she had a real talent for writing and thought she could have gone on to do big things but Dad got in her way and distracted her then got her pregnant and then led her down a pathway to her current life, a widow in her late thirties, working as an administrator in a law firm in Reading, and coping with me and all my stuff. I suppose if Uncle Edward had a time machine he would travel back to the night Mum and Dad met and made sure she never laid eyes on him. But then I wouldn't exist either so I suppose I'm glad they did meet. And Uncle Edward came round eventually and accepted things the way they were, but I think he was sort of glad when they got divorced, although he never said so. Dad's rows with Mum were to blame but that was mainly when he'd had too much to drink and that was only because he needed some outlet for his feelings, things he'd seen and stuff. He told me about some of them sometimes, when he was drunk and Mum had gone to bed and I'd sneaked downstairs in our old house to get a glass of water but really just to check that he was OK, 'cos I'd heard about people choking on their own vomit when they were drunk and didn't want that to happen to him, although I did want him to stop drinking so much, and stop rowing with Mum and stop putting himself through all that shit. But that was him and when he wasn't like that he was a brilliant Dad and always made me laugh and did cool things with me and taught me to swim. He was going to teach me to drive, too. But I guess I'll have to get lessons now as I don't really fancy having Mum or Uncle Edward do it.

'Natasha's looking fit in that dress,' Ash said. 'She was at Ayesha's 16th birthday party in September when these were taken. Look, there's me with Steve and Alan. God, what was Steve wearing? He looks a right muppet. I can't see you in any of ....' He suddenly stopped, realizing what he was about to say.

'That was just about a fortnight after we'd buried my Dad. I guess I wasn't in the partying mood just then. But it's good to see everyone else was, though.'

'God, Andrew, I'm really sorry, I just...'

'Forgot, I know, don't sweat it, Ash. It's not like it was any big deal for anyone but me anyway, was it?' I could feel my voice getting angry but I couldn't help it.

'It's not that, Andrew. We were all upset by your loss.' The last word sounded heavy and alien in Ash's mouth. 'Natasha cried so much when she heard about it, for you, y'know. We all know how close you were to him. And we all respect him, y'know. He died a hero, died for his country, and stuff.'

I had to stay silent because I knew I would explode if someone told me that once more. I didn't care about that; all I knew was that my Dad was gone.

'It was a crap party, anyway,' Ash started up again, changing the mood. 'Ayesha got drunk on the punch 'cos someone laced it with vodka or gin or something, and barfed all over Kelly Reilly's dress. Actually, that was an improvement on what she'd been wearing.'

We both laughed and that helped the mood, a bit. But it made me realise that while I'd been going through all this stuff, everyone else had just been getting on with their lives, going to school, going to parties, having boyfriends and girlfriends, having fights and making up. All the time my world had stopped spinning, everyone else's just went on turning as if nothing had happened. And that didn't seem fair, somehow.

I lay on my bed and stared at the ceiling.

'Are you religious, Ash?' The words hung there between us like something violated. I could hear that he'd stopped tapping on the keyboard but he didn't answer, not straight away.

'Well, y'know, sort of, I suppose. I don't think about it. I go to mosque with Dad and my brothers and stuff. I suppose everyone needs a code of ethics to live by, and the Qur'an is as good a one as any, I mean, that it's the word of..... well, y'know, don't make me talk about this stuff, I'm not really comfortable with it. I mean, I'm not embarrassed or ashamed of it or anything but I don't really want to have this sort of conversation with you, it's just too weird, man.'

'I don't mean do you believe in the rules and stuff. I mean do you really believe in life after death, in Heaven, in a supreme being who created the universe, all that stuff?'

'Well, I don't really know.'

'But you're a scientist, Ash. That's what you keep telling me, you bang on for hours about quantum physics and how we're on the brink of understanding more than we thought was possible about the universe. Don't you think that does away with God?'

Ash stumbled over his reply, clearly uncomfortable. 'Well, science and faith aren't really the same things, y'know. But they're not mutually exclusive, are they? You can be an empirical scientist and still have room for faith, can't you? Science is about the pursuit of truth through empirical study of physical nature, and faith is about accepting that some things are beyond our understanding, that we can never know. But we can accept or even be grateful that it exists. That God exists.'

'I used to think something like that, when I was younger, and I suppose I still do, or want to, or something. It's a nice thought, isn't it, the idea of someone watching over us, that somehow we're important in the bigger scheme of things, that our lives matter, and we're going to get our reward for a well-lived life. But lately I don't think like that anymore. Lately, I think that nobody is watching over us, that we're on our own, to mess things up without divine intervention, to kill and maim each other. The only laughable thing about it all is that people claim to kill in the name of God or Allah or Buddha or whatever, all the time. Even people who believe in the same God, like Catholics and Protestants, like my Gran who had to leave Northern Ireland 'cos she married a Protestant, like anyone could even tell you what the difference is really. It doesn't matter to anyone at all but for her and Granddad it meant leaving a country they both loved to come to England and live among strangers. They never went back to Ireland when my Granddad was alive, can you believe that? Gran and Mum took his ashes back and scattered them somewhere over there. Hard to credit it really, isn't it? But these are the consequences of people's blind belief that God is one their side, that they'll get their reward in Heaven, or Nirvana or Valhalla or wherever.'

Ash started typing again after waiting for a moment, then said something about religions not being responsible for the actions of their followers and with that closed down the whole conversation. I sensed I'd strayed too close to something like offending him. I realised then that we never really had a conversation like this before, even though we'd spoken almost every day since beginning secondary school together, even though we had religious education classes together. The school was Catholic in ethos but of course accepted others, at least in small numbers, just to avoid looking too exclusive or even racist, possibly. Although, in fairness, they did take time to explain different religions to us, not just Christianity or Catholicism. My Gran had a dim view about things like that, saying she thought it was all well and good admitting 'all sorts' to a good Catholic school as long as they didn't forget it was a Catholic school. She could be quite racist without even meaning to be in that sort of casual way older people can be although in her life she never treated anyone differently because of their race or religion, not that I'd seen anyway. In fact, when she did talk about these things at all, which was not that often, she used to say how no matter what part of the world you were in you could go into a Catholic church and take part in the Mass without even needing to speak the language, because it was the universal church and that it lived the concept fully. In the old days when all Catholic masses were in Latin the world was even more united, she said, but I thought that was mainly because it meant that no one anywhere could understand what was being said except the priests as it was unlikely the congregation in Brazil or Malaysia or Mexico could speak Latin. But women like my Gran the world over brought their troubles to the feet of statues of the Virgin Mary and cried prayers into blinking candles, clicking Rosary beads and hoping the Mother of Christ would have sympathy for them and their troubles with their children and how the world treated them. And if these women were anything like my Gran then they really believed the Mother of God was listening and would even answer their prayers on occasion, whether it was to help me pass an exam or get me through the death of my father. They did not doubt. They believed. And they believed that people who'd 'passed on' still lived on in our lives, affecting us, and exerting a benign influence, watching over us, becoming our own guardian angels, waiting patiently until we met again. And that thought was so powerful that it shaped entire lives, entire cultures and gave solace to legions of mothers who lost sons or husbands in millennia of wars and conflicts. And who was worse off having that faith in their lives? Were they fools breathing their prayers into the uncaring wind or women who knew that all their suffering in this vale of tears would all make sense some day if only they kept the faith. So how could you resist this siren call of certainty and yet how did we all lose this certainty, replacing it with an emptiness and finality with no hope of redemption. In my world, my Dad was dead, never to be with me again, gone forever, never to be involved in my life on earth ever again, leaving me alone with no one to watch over me. In my Gran's world, no one was ever given more burdens than they could carry by God who tested them to elevate them to be the best that they could be and so earn their place in Heaven where they would be once again with all those people they had loved and lost. So who was worse off and who felt the loss more acutely? And did those men who planted that bomb that killed my Dad and wounded the men with him believe they moved closer to their God in doing this act? And did their children glow with pride when they heard of their fathers' deeds? And did their wives smile on hearing how they had triumphed over the infidel invaders? Or did some boy somewhere also grieve for his dead father like me without any comfort that they would meet again in some great hereafter, or think about how the loss inflicted on the 'enemy' would leave a family bereft and fatherless and blight the lives of all who knew the man their father had killed?

A thought then jumped into my head, unbeckoned, unwanted, and unneeded but absolutely urgently, insistently, powerfully: had I had a religious experience? Had the Maiwand Lion been some sort of message to me, from God, from my father? Some divine clue that the man who had been the most important person in my life had not truly died, that he did still exist, still watched over me. And once I thought this, once I'd allowed the thought to manifest itself, it burst through all my doubt and debate with irresistible force. It demanded that I think again, really think again about what I had witnessed. And that was the word, I realised. I had witnessed something phenomenal, something out of the ordinary, something supernatural. The doctors couldn't tell me what had happened to cause me to collapse. I did not believe it was simply an emotional reaction as the mad shrink seemed to think. I knew I had seen something with my eyes that was as real as anything I had ever seen or will do until I die. And I felt the roar of this creature reverberate in my chest so hard it made my heart skip beats. And I saw it look at me, directly, right in my eyes. It looked at me and spoke to me. I was just too stupid and scared at the time to realise it. I had experienced an apparition, a message from God. The lion roared its message to me and I had not listened. I had been overcome by disbelief, just like those prophets in the Bible who don't believe they were witnessing a message from God when He called them the first time. And maybe that was what being human meant, that we looked for the mundane instead of the divine in all the things we see and hear. But could this really be? And yet, in the absence of any other explanation, why not? The Maiwand Lion was a war memorial, commemorating the deaths of British soldiers killed in Afghanistan, just like my father had been killed. He too had died bravely at the hands of a cowardly enemy. So where better to manifest yourself if you too had died in action than the monument to the older war in the same place? And now that the thought took hold of me, it wouldn't let go. I could feel my heart racing, felt breathless, felt lightheaded. I wanted to cry out, to say something, but what, and who could I tell without sounding mad? And did I really believe what I was now thinking?

I looked over towards Ash, he had stopped typing on the keyboard and slowly swivelled around to look at me. For a moment, I swear, I thought he could read my mind, the look on his face was so intense and serious.

'I do believe in God,' he said, slowly and solemnly. 'I do believe in Heaven, and an afterlife and all that stuff. I should never have let you think I didn't. My faith is part of who I am and I'm not ashamed of it. It makes me a better person and it doesn't make me less of a scientist. There's room for both. I just wanted to say that to you, so you know, that's all.'

I sat forward on the bed and looked at him, seeing him look so serious and almost as if I'd never really looked at him so closely before. 'I know, Ash.'

CHAPTER FIVE

Confession

The next time I was due to see Dr. Medusa was an afternoon appointment in early December. The weather was turning very cold by then and Gran, who was being given a lift by Mum as far as St. James's Church, complained that it was 'a lazy wind blowing, it'd rather go through you than round you.' We laughed at her funny saying, her Irish accent always a lot thicker when she reeled off all those phrases she'd probably heard a lot back in Ireland when she was growing up. She was well muffled up against the wind anyway, with her fur collar turned up, her fur hat pulled down and a black woollen scarf wrapped tightly around her throat. All her clothes were black which only added to the pallor of her face and the luminosity of her blue eyes which shone more brightly than any woman of her age I'd ever seen before. Mum looked at her in the rear-view mirror as we drove along, the traffic relatively light in the early afternoon.

'I'll drop you off by the prison, if that's all right, Mum.'

'Thanks, luv, that's grand. I don't mind so long as I don't have to spend too much time walking around in this weather, it's perishin' cold, so it is. Fr. Murphy doesn't keep the church what I'd call over-heated either, so I hope I don't get too cold before I get in and settled.' She pulled her collar even closer to her face, as if to suck up the last of the heat from the car before braving the cold air outside as we pulled up right beside the prison, next door to the church and adjacent to the Forbury Gardens, where the Maiwand Lion stood.

'What is it again you're doing here, Mum?'

'Ah, just going to confession, is all. It's Advent now so I won't get a chance again before Christmas.'

'What sins to you have to confess, Gran?' I scoffed. 'Have you been shop-lifting Werther's Originals again?'

Mum laughed but stifled it quickly and hissed my name in admonition. But Gran was used to my humour and came back just as quick.

'Very funny, young fella but believe you and me that there's plenty goes on in my life I don't want on the balance sheet when I check-in. Anyway, it's a good chance to get it all off your chest and a damn sight cheaper and easier than some ways I could think of.' The last comment was a loaded reference to the fact we were off to see Dr. Medusa again. Mum glanced at Gran in the rear-view mirror, reprimanding her with her eyes, brusquely announcing they were here now so she'd better get up before they caused a traffic jam.

'All right, all right, I'm goin'. I'll say a prayer from you while I'm here. And don't worry about picking me up later. I'm meeting Margaret for tea in town in a while and she'll drop me off home.'

We waved good-bye and soon were whizzing by the Forbury Gardens. I couldn't help but fix my gaze on the Maiwand Lion, his huge bulk clearly visible from the road, through the few trees denuded of leaves at this time of year.

'Why do you think Gran is so obsessed with all that religious stuff?'

'God knows, Andrew.' Mum had little patience with it all and it had always been a bone of contention between the two of them. 'I suppose it gives her something in her life, some comfort or something. Probably the way she grew up in Ireland. Back then stuff like that was really important. I suppose when it gets you when you're young like that then it sticks.'

'But it didn't stick with you, did it, though?'

'No, I s'ppose not.' She smiled a little, thinking back to her childhood perhaps. 'Your Gran would say that's proof positive of the damage growing up in a heathen country does.'

I smiled too 'cause I knew this was a favourite phrase of Gran's. She was always complaining that when people lost their god then they lost their way. 'You can say what you like about the Muslims and Hindus and Sikhs and what have you,' she'd say summing up the sagacity of her seniority. 'But at least they *believe* in something. When you stop believing in something bigger than yourself, when you think that you're the centre of the universe, well, it's not long before you start losing all sense of your place in the scheme of things. People who stop believing in God start believing in any old stuff, new age crap and crystals and all sorts of claptrap.'

I knew Gran put attending a psychologist into this same category. I knew she thought there was nothing wrong with me that time couldn't fix. She often said that God had a plan for us all and that he wouldn't give us a cross to carry we couldn't bear; that suffering was part of the human condition and with His good grace I was getting my share out of the way early, so I could look forward to being stronger and a better person once I 'got over' this 'great loss'. 'Time is a great healer, Andrew,' she'd say, 'and time will bring us all together with those we've lost in due course.' She totally believed this. It was said with such certainty you sort of believed it too, for a while anyway. But as we swung by the Maiwand Lion, great grey mass of iron, stood there, still like a tightened bow, I thought that perhaps there might be more truth in her world than mine. In her world, miracles happened. In her world, statues moved, wept tears of blood, apparitions happened, angels and saints brought messages from the other world to this one. In her world, I wouldn't be so messed up about what had happened to me. I'd probably just accept it that God was trying to speak to me, through the lion, like Aslan in Narnia. I'd probably be more interested about what he was trying to tell me than whether it had happened or not. And maybe that was my real problem. Maybe my lack of faith in what I'd seen was the issue. I'd witnessed a *bona fide* miracle and all I could do was wonder what was wrong with me. Although that was what often happened when people saw miracles, Gran said. She said St. Bernadette was tormented all her life by people doubting her, thinking she was mad, an 'attention-seeker' we'd say today. But she never lost her faith that she had witnessed a miracle and she had seen the Mother of God in a grotto in a grotty little village in France. And those girls who saw the Virgin Mary in Medjugorje saw her regularly, held conversations with her, witnessed by thousands. Although no one else could see what they saw it didn't stop millions of people flocking to them just to be near the miraculous. Gran had been one of them, joining a bunch of other old biddies on a pilgrimage on her first ever trip abroad aboard an airplane to travel to a country that didn't exist anymore just before it descended into bloodshed. Maybe that's the message, the warning, that these things happen at times and in places where really bad things are about to take place. And maybe that was what was going on with me too. Maybe something really bad was going to happen to me. Maybe my vision was a brain tumour they hadn't found on my MRI scan.

I was aware we were at Dr. Medusa's place only when Mum pulled up to a parking space beside the office.

'Bit of luck that,' she smiled, 'finding a parking space right where we're going. I thought we'd have to go round to Sidmouth Street and walk round in the cold. Maybe it's my lucky day.'

'Maybe you should buy a lottery ticket, then. I could do with an X-Box for Christmas.'

She smiled that we'd see what Santa brought and it would depend on whether I'd been a good boy that year. She then suddenly realised what she'd said, what year we'd just gone through. It rested there between us for a few seconds. I could have said something, something to hurt her, maybe. But I decided to ignore it. What was the point? She'd had a crap year too, one way or the other, I'd guessed.

Dr. Medusa was dressed exactly as she had been the last time I met her, down to the thick woollen tights which barely contained the sausage of her calves. Her office was the usual mess, various things scattered around on all available surfaces. We had to move a newspaper to make room to sit down on the couch.

'O dear me, I do apologise! What am I like, Kathryn? You must think I'm a complete slob!' she apologised effusively, a bit am-dram if you ask me.

'Don't worry,' Mum answered politely. 'I live with a teenage boy, don't forget, so I'm use to a bit of clutter!'

Dr. Medusa chuckled, looked at me with something like amused affection, saying she supposed that was very true.

'I'm quite tidy, actually,' I protested. I'm no slob. I'm like Dad like that. He couldn't abide mess. Said that you wasted more time looking for things in a cluttered place than it took to tidy them away properly in the first place. It was probably his military training and stuff. Mum was the only slob in our house. Since Dad left, the state of our house took a nose-dive. If it wasn't for Gran nagging her, Mum would be quite happy to live like a slob, I reckon.

'Can I get either of you a cup of tea or coffee, perhaps?'

'No, thanks,' I answered. She'd probably add it to the bill, I thought and I wasn't sure I wanted to drink anything from any cup she'd been involved in washing from the look of her cardigan, which carried stains like an artist's palette.

Mum said we were both fine for drinks, thank you. Dr. Medusa confided that she drank far too much coffee than was healthy but as it was her only remaining vice she felt entitled. From the size of her backside, I reckoned she liked to have a cake or two with those coffees too so gluttony obviously wasn't seen as a vice in her eyes.

She parked her ample arse into the armchair now moulded through years of use to a perfect match. She smiled at us, sitting there, waiting, as if we were supposed to start or something. Eventually, she asked how we both were. I shrugged, Mum said we were both well, thank you.

'Really?' asked Medusa, staring at us intently, her old crone eyes fixing on me. 'Isn't that great, then? Job done- that was easy!' She laughed to indicate she was obviously joking but I took my cue from that opening.

'Well, there was nothing wrong with me in the first place, was there? So there was nothing really for you to do, really.'

'Andrew!' Mum reprimanded me. She was always in a flap if she felt I was being in anyway disrespectful to anyone in any sort of authority role. It got on my wick.

'What?' I snapped. 'I told you there was nothing wrong with me, nothing that wasn't normal, anyway. I don't see why we have to continue with this stuff when there is nothing to do.'

'Well, Andrew,' Medusa mused moving forward in her chair to stare right into my face. 'I agree with you. There is clearly nothing wrong with you requiring my services. I think you're a lovely, normal healthy young man. You've been through a lot of things, your Mum and you, great loss, but you're coping really well with it all. You're a credit to your Dad. I'm sure he would be very proud of you and how you've handled yourself, don't you?'

Cheap trick, I thought. Using that comment about Dad and how he'd feel about me. No matter how I tried, it always sort of got me, made my voice catch, get stuck in my throat, like someone grabbed me there. I tried to say something smart but it just came out as a sort of squeak so I shrugged my shoulders. Medusa smiled benignly, seeing her shots hit home, just as she'd intended, crafty old cow.

'And you should be very proud of Andrew, Kathryn.' She moved her attention to Mum now, who was confused, not knowing whether she should accept the compliment or concern herself with comforting me.

'I am,' she said quietly but confidently. 'I really am. He's been amazing.

He's coped with so many things so well. I know it's been hard for him at times. But I know he knows his family loves him and that we're all there for him.' She squeezed my hand. It felt sort of nice, I have to admit. Her hand felt warm and soft and familiar.

'Well, we're all agreed, then,' Medusa summed up, straightening her back, her large breasts rising as she did so, making her look like one of those things you see on the prow of an old ship. 'Great work, everyone. A new record for me, too. I'm delighted. I've been doing this sort of work for donkey's years now and I've never had such a speedy conclusion. Case closed. Everyone can just get on with their lives now, can't they? All the better for our time together, I'd say. Listen, Kathryn, why don't you go and speak to my secretary while Andrew and I compare notes?' She stood up and took Mum by the hand, virtually giving her the bum's rush out of the room. Mum looked confused, I could see it in her eyes but before I could really get a grip on what was happening she was gone, the door closed behind her and Medusa was standing there, leaning against the closed door, smiling, like she'd just gotten rid of an unwelcome guest who'd overstayed their welcome.

'Well, now, Andrew. We can have a final little chat before I send you on your way, too.'

She sat down beside me, literally, on the same couch. I sort of bounced a little while she settled her big backside down on it beside me. She placed her hand on my arm. It didn't feel natural. I flinched a little.

'Don't worry, my boy, I'm not going to bite!' She laughed heartily at her own joke. 'I just thought that, between the two of us and the gatepost, we could just come clean, as it were. I mean, I know you're a clever lad, and I know you don't need anything from me but I am just curious about what really happened, you know? Just professional curiosity, as it were. Just level with me. What do you think really happened to you that day, Remembrance Sunday? I mean, we both know, don't we, that you didn't have a seizure or faint because you hadn't eaten something for breakfast? You're an intelligent lad and you want to become a doctor yourself, don't you? So you'll appreciate the interest of a colleague in a case like this? And I know you're too clever to ignore a problem that could be really serious, aren't you? I mean, how would that look, an aspiring young medic ignoring signs of a major medical problem, and all? So my theory is, and I'll share it with you, that you saw something or perhaps heard something that morning, witnessed something, you might say, which scared the living wits out of you? Am I right? Something that made so little sense that your brain could do nothing other than reject it? And that caused your little episode, didn't it, Andrew? Am I right? I am right, aren't I? Just let me know, you know, doctor to doctor, as it were. It would really help me to know I'm not losing my touch, you know. I mean, what if I meet someone less clever and capable as you as a patient in the future, it would really help me help them to know whether I'm right or wrong. It could really make a difference to someone else, to their care. You understand that, Andrew, don't you. Tell me I'm right. Go on. No one else needs to know anything about it. Whatever it was you're clearly over it so I don't think we need worry anymore, do we? What did you see, Andrew? What did you see? Was it your father, Andrew? Did you see your father there, among those soldiers, all lined up by the war memorial that morning? Did you Andrew?'

I shook my head. Her words, the grip she had on my arm, it all made my head swim. It was like she was in my brain, rooting around in there. Then she said that I'd seen my father. I mean, how stupid was that, I didn't see my Dad. Why would she say that? Why would she say that? If I saw my Dad I would have been delighted. I would have run over to see him properly, to touch him. No, I didn't see my bloody father.

'No, no,' I stammered. 'I didn't see my Dad.'

'But you saw something, Andrew. Didn't you? What did you see, Andrew? Please tell me, please? I won't say a word to anyone but I really need to know. Please. Andrew. What did you see?'

'The lion. I saw the lion, OK? I saw the lion.'

'The lion? What do you mean? O, do you mean that big iron statue in the park?'

I nodded. I couldn't help it. It was out now. I could feel the urge to tell her everything rising in my chest. I could feel her hand on my arm urging me to tell her, tell her everything. And I wanted to. I really did. I don't know why I did but I did.

'The Maiwand Lion. That's what it's called.'

'Ah, yes- I remember now. But what about it, what did you see, exactly?'

'I saw it move.'

A silence followed, for a moment or two, and I felt her hand on my arm and I felt my hand was trembling, shaking, in fact, my whole body was shaking. Like I was cold. But I wasn't. I felt too warm, if anything. I could feel my face flush, I could feel some sweat prickle on my forehead and on my upper lip.

'How did it move, Andrew?' That's what she asked me. Not what the hell did I mean, I saw a statue move. No, she asked me how it moved.

'Well, it sort of turned its head or something. Y'know, it turned its head. It was looking away from me, from where I was standing. And then it sort of turned to look at me.' I couldn't look in her eyes but I felt them staring intently at me. Her face came closer to mine. I could smell the coffee on her breath. I could feel her hand move on my arm, stroking me, like she was soothing me.

'And what else, Andrew. Did you hear anything? Feel anything?'

I answered really slowly, my voice almost whispering. 'I thought I heard it roar. I heard it roar. It opened its mouth, while it was looking straight at me, and roared. It roared at me, like that lion at the start of the movies or something.'

'And how did you feel, Andrew. How do you feel when you saw this, heard this?'

I looked at her straight in the face now. I could feel tears welling up in my eyes. I don't know why. I seemed to tear up over nothing those days, usually when someone was talking about my Dad. But that time we were just talking about the lion, something I'd thought about every single day since it had happened. I looked at her straight in the face, with tears in my eyes and all, and croaked, whispered:

'I was frightened.'

'Go on,' she whispered. 'What else did you feel?'

'I thought maybe I was going to die. That the lion was there to kill me. That I was going to be dead, like my Dad.'

Then my voice just stopped working. And I could feel my whole body shake, like I was really shuddering. And then these sobs, I guess you'd call them, just came up from deep within my chest and shook me. I didn't even sound like me. I didn't know why I was acting like this. I sort out saw myself as if I was watching myself. I saw myself sitting there on the edge of this battered couch, this old fat woman sitting there beside me, putting her arm over my shoulder and stroking my forearm with her other hand. Comforting me, like I was her kid or something.

'Have you told anyone about this, Andrew?' she asked, her voice soft and steady. I shook my head to say no because I don't think I could speak.

'Not your Mum?' I shook my head even more vigorously.

'How about a friend maybe? Have you confided in any of your friends?'

I found my voice then. 'No way! They'd think I was crazy or something!'

'And do you think you're crazy, Andrew?'

I paused. How could I answer that question? Part of me did think I was going mad but another part had started to believe that maybe I had seen a miracle or something, a special message meant only for me. I just didn't understand yet what it meant. Eventually, I said no, I didn't think so. But I did know something funny had happened to me. That I was worried about myself a little. I thought maybe something bad was going to happen to me. Then I sort of ran out of steam. Stopped dead.

'Do you mean something bad like what happened to your father, Andrew?' she asked, patiently.

I shrugged. Maybe, I don't know.

'But Andrew, your father was killed in the line of duty. He was a soldier. I know it's very hard for you, for any of us, to understand or accept. But he willingly put himself in harm's way, because he was a professional soldier, dedicated to his job, and his country, I dare say. While it's very sad what happened to him, it doesn't mean that you are going to come to any harm. The two things are not connected. Do you understand?'

I shrugged, said yeah, I know, sort of but bad things happen to good people all the time. You don't have to be a soldier in a war to die.

'No, you don't, Andrew. You're quite correct. But sometimes when we lose someone very close to us we feel a little bit more vulnerable ourselves. Because death has touched us somehow and that makes us feel less secure in ourselves, in our own lives.'

'I've experienced death before, though,' I retorted. 'My grand-Dad died when I was about eight. He had a type of lung cancer he got from working with asbestos, years ago, in the shipyards of Belfast, they think. So I know what it feels like to lose someone. But I've never felt like this before.'

'Well, sometimes it's the unexpectedness or the suddenness of dying that upsets us more than the fact of death itself. Especially if we've not had the chance to say goodbye to the person who died because we didn't think we needed to do so, because we assumed we would see them again.'

The last words hung in the air between us, like her stale coffee breath. No time to say good-bye. That was true. I didn't have a chance to say goodbye. When he was last home, Dad had been drinking a lot more than normal. He turned up unannounced at our house one night, saying he wanted to see me, see his son. Mum was incensed, told him he was in a right state and that he had no right to turn up let that, especially so late at night, demanding to see me. She said that I was in bed. But I wasn't. I was on the landing, watching them argue. She was holding the door slightly ajar but making sure he couldn't get in. All I could hear was his voice: obviously drunk, pleading initially, begging then, switching to aggressive and demanding when he saw my Mum was not to be moved. Then the bang on the door, his fist, my mother's grip momentarily lost, my father's face, red and angry, glaring at her with hatred, then his eyes scanning then up to meet mine.

'Andrew, Andy, my wee boy. Come and say hello to your old man, eh?'

Mum protesting, trying to wrestle the door closed again, him, strong, resisting her. Then me, shouting, stop it, stop it, Dad. Leave Mum alone. Get out!

Then more shouts, anger. Him, accusing her of turning me against him, turning me into a 'bloody Mamma's boy'. He didn't care I heard that. That's what he really thought of me. Mum riled now, screaming at him, threatening to call the police, telling him just to go, no one wanted him here. Him, cursing her, saying she'd taken everything from him he cared for, his home, his family. That he might as well be dead for all she cared. That was May, the last time I saw him. Before deployment. He was dead just over two months later.

'I need to go now, OK?' I shook Medusa's hand from my arm, stood up, and left, without looking back, in case her look caught my eye, in case I turned to jelly not stone.

CHAPTER SIX

Advent

The weather turned even colder, one of the coldest Decembers in Britain on record, they said. Everything froze, icy-white, dead. The leafless trees etched scratches onto the low winter sky. Darkness and coldness prevailed and the sun sank low in the sky as we slid towards the solstice.

I couldn't concentrate at school, even in the subjects I liked, like English. Brennan droning on like he did. I'd never noticed before how heavy-handed and hammy he was reading the text. Perhaps the meaning of the words never mattered before to me, not really. But that term we were doing *Hamlet*. The dead king goading his son to avenge his unnatural death from beyond the grave. The son hesitating because of conscience or cowardice or concerns for evidence, to assure himself that he had not simply imagined the whole thing, that the message to kill Claudius wasn't simply the workings of his fucked-up mind but was truthful. *The play's the thing wherein we catch the conscience of the king.* I wouldn't have had any need for proof that my father had been murdered nor any hesitation in dispatching his killers from this world into the next if given half a chance. Of course, it was easy for me to think that sitting there in English class in Reading, fantasising about how to wreak my revenge on those faceless killers, the Taliban. Mainly because there was no way I was ever going to be in a situation where I could do anything about it. But I felt like it was my duty or something to at least hate them. Although if I told the truth to myself, I was finding it harder and harder to hold onto the hatred. It consumed so much time and energy and stuff was happening to me here and now that I needed to pay attention to. I felt like my resolve was weakening or something, and then I hated myself even more because I was letting my Dad down.

I couldn't even be the sort of son to carry hatred in his heart for his murderers. What a waste of space.

Brennan talked about how the conflict between Gertrude and Hamlet was the pivotal point of the play in his opinion, as it allowed Hamlet to vent his spleen on his mother, the person he really blamed in the whole thing, more so even than Claudius because he had loved and respected his mother and when she betrayed that love the betrayal was a lot harder to bear than that of Claudius who we never feel was ever close to Hamlet or vice-versa. I could understand that, could see why Hamlet would hate his mother, because she had so quickly replaced his father in her heart and in her bed. Brennan maintained that this relationship was what drove the play. The conflict between mother and son, the almost Oedipal nature of their relationship. We had a lot of laughs asking him to explain what he meant by that, seeing him stammer and fluster and blush, blathering on about Greek mythology while someone shouted 'motherfucker' under a cough. The class erupted into laughter. I didn't laugh, well not much anyway. I felt sorry for Brennan actually. He stopped the class until whoever had done it owned up. Of course, no one did. And the stand-off just made him look impotent. So he stormed out and we were left to our own devices until he came back, about ten minutes later. We thought he was going to give us all detention or something. But he just carried on as if nothing had happened. We stared at each other. Natasha smiled at me. I smiled back, not knowing why really. Ash just carried on reading his text without glancing around. I knew he thought things like that were immature and stupid. So did I really, but I was in that sort of mood then. I think I found Brennan's well-rehearsed and over-used phrases tiresome. I suppose that's want happens teachers. They become inured to the words they read year in, year out, to a bunch of adolescents who are only there because they have to be. But underneath all of that, I think I understood Hamlet. I felt his impotent rage. I understood his hatred of his mother and his step-father. I understood his horror when confronted with the ghost of his father. Perhaps because I had been given a 'visitation' or whatever that was I had seen in Forbury Gardens a month before.

I didn't go back to see Medusa since I told her about what I had seen, even though she had told my mother that she did need to see me. She didn't tell her why exactly, doctor-patient confidentiality and all that. But she did say I needed more sessions with her and that we'd made a breakthrough last time after she'd left us alone. I didn't want to see her again though so I fobbed her off. They even tried to get Uncle Edward in on the act to strong-arm me into submission. He tried to reason with me. Told me that whatever the shrink had uncovered was probably very important for me to deal with. That if I didn't then maybe I could have further 'episodes' or even worse. But I lied to him. I told him I didn't know what she had told him but that I felt fine and that he was just wasting his money paying for her, that she was a charlatan just trying to screw more money out of us. He looked disappointed by my response and clearly didn't believe me. But he said that it was my decision, that he realised I was old enough and bright enough to manage my own health 'issues'. But he cautioned me about ignoring the advice of professionals trying to help me because they have no vested interest except to help me. And that the money thing was irrelevant anyway as it came out of his private health insurance so I didn't need to worry on that account. I told him I understood he was trying to help me but that I felt a lot better than I had done before when I had my 'episode' and that I didn't need any more help. But that wasn't true.

The truth was that the lion visited me often, in idle moments in the day, in the last minutes of consciousness before sleep, in my dreams, or nightmares and in the first thoughts in my head when I awoke. The lion gnawed away at my heart and at my mind. It came to be the thing at the centre of me, that thing which became the driving force of my life. I could not settle on anything, I could not think about anything else. What had I seen? What did it mean? Had I really seen anything at all or was it just a dream, or hallucination or an over-active imagination? It would be better to be any of those things than what occurred to me more and more, that it was a visitation. I felt stupid even saying the word, even to myself. It sounded so 'medieval', so religious, so ridiculous. And yet, and yet, and yet... I could not move beyond it. I could not move on from the thought that what I had seen had meaning, had significance, that it meant something. I simply wasn't bright enough to 'decode' the meaning. That's what it had become, a puzzle to solve. But who had set the cryptic clue for me to ponder? God? The Devil? The universe? No one?

I could feel the pressure to ask advice build up in my chest. But I was scared of the consequences. I had told Medusa and look what she'd done. Started to badger me into coming in to see her again. Clearly, she thought I was crazy, certifiable, probably literally. But I did not feel crazy. I knew what I had seen was real and that it was meant for me to see. Maybe, it was even a sign from my Dad. Imagine that, a signal from where he was to where I was to tell me not to be afraid, that I was not alone. But I had no real language to use to describe such things. Even to say them out loud was scary to me because I would have to admit my feelings as well as my thoughts, tell someone what I thought it meant, hoped it meant and that would expose me to lots of 'interventions' I did not want, or need.

And so I sat at my computer screen, staring at the text I had written for my English essay, on the question of the significance of the supernatural in the play *Hamlet*. I had looked at the notes I'd made in Brennan's class and my text books. But none of these figured in my answer. I had written that the appearance of the ghost of Hamlet's father was to signify the importance of the need for action in this world because the crime committed had 'cried out to Heaven' for vengeance. There could be no peace in the other world until justice had been served in this one. And Hamlet's dead father could not find peace until his killer had been killed. The situation was so important that it tore through the fabric between the worlds and manifested itself in the form of Hamlet's father's ghost. I realised then what the meaning of the lion's roar had been. The unnatural killing of my father, his replacement so quickly in my mother's affections, and perhaps even his absence from my life too. How quickly I had tried to 'get back to normal' after his death. I even felt embarrassed by condolences. I shrugged them off as if the whole thing was an unnecessary fuss about nothing. I had not even said good-bye to him before he left.

Ash was working beside me in the school library. We usually sat beside each other. Mainly because no one else wanted to sit beside us. But also because we both had a similar work ethic and used the time to get on with homework and study rather than chat together like the others. Natasha sometimes sat with us especially lately but she wasn't there that day because she'd arranged to go Christmas shopping with her Mum after school as it was late night opening in town. I hadn't even started my shopping yet. This was the first year I wouldn't have to buy anything for Dad. And that made it really difficult for me to even think about shopping at all. And Mum and I were at each other's throat all the time lately. She'd been seeing that plonker from work more and more. I came home from Ash's last Friday evening to find him sitting there, in the living room. Said he was waiting from Mum to change, that she was upstairs, that they were going to the 'office Chrimbo shindig', he actually said that- what a dick! I just said, whatever or something, and went to the kitchen to get a bowl of *Kellogg's Crunchy Nut Cornflakes*. But I was really pissed off to find him sitting in our living room, watching TV like he owned the place, done up like a Pound Shop James Bond in his Mr. Buyright monkey suit. I couldn't remember Mum even saying she was going out that night. But then we communicated mainly via Post-It notes on the fridge these days. I hung out with Ash after school then his Dad would drive me home if it was late. I envied Ash his normal life. Mum, Dad, brother and sisters. All together in their little house, always glad to see each other, friendly bickering about stuff.

Mum didn't see I was standing in the kitchen when she came down the stairs, all tarted up like a Russian hooker, a new red dress, her hair done up, her high heels on, full make-up. And then him, taking her hands in his, kissing her on the lips, telling her she looked wonderful. Enough to make you puke, smarmy bastard. She then realised I was standing there, in the kitchen, holding a bowl in one hand and a spoon in the other, just staring at them.

'Andrew, you're home. I've left some food in the fridge for you, you just have to heat it up. We're going to the office party tonight, remember?'

I didn't answer, just shrugged. I slurped the milk from my spoon loudly.

'Well, we should probably go, darling.' Darling, that's what she called him, darling, bloody *darling*. I could feel my blood boil.

'Yeah, why don't you go, both of you, before I barf!' I shouted at them.

'Andrew!' Mum glared at me. Then she apologised to the dickhead, who just told her he was sure I was just 'messing around' and that seeing 'two oldies like us canoodling' must be 'disconcerting to say the least', chortling to himself like he was funny or something.

Then he helped Mum into her good winter coat and she tucked her red velvet scarf around her neck before saying good-night and 'don't wait up', like she was funny or something. Then they both left and I was standing there, by myself, in the kitchen, again. I didn't see her until the following afternoon 'cos she wasn't there when I got up in the morning and went into town. We hadn't spoken to each other since then. Or at least I hadn't spoken to her. It was clear what they'd been up to and it made me sick. Hard to stomach when your mother's a slag.

So that week I'd spent as long as possible in school before getting the bus back to Ash's house and usually eating with his family. His Mum didn't mind. She cooked loads of food and said one extra mouth was no problem. I think she felt sorry for me. She was maternal and all that, probably why she'd had so many kids. Not like my mother. I always felt like she resented me or something, like I'd ruined her life by being born, got in the way of her making something of her life. Me and my Dad, two big disappointments for her. At least my Dad was out of the way now. And I planned to be so as soon as I could.

Ash asked if I wanted to come to his house again tonight. If that's alright, I answered. Yeah, course it is, he said. He got some new *Doctor Who* DVDs from Amazon that morning so we could watch some episodes if we wanted after dinner.

We walked from the school towards the town centre. It was freezing. Our breath hung in the air before us as we walked and talked. Christmas lights up everywhere. Frost on the ground, twinkling under the street lamps. Ice where puddles used to be, the ground rock-hard on the grassy bits between the pavements and the road. Ash rattled on about *Doctor Who*. I didn't mind, it was nice to hear something else but the thoughts in my head recently. He decoded each episode like it was the Enigma Code or something: what the significance of different plotlines and characters were, how they related to other characters and the 'story arc' over nearly sixty years or something. He could find enough to talk about for half an hour in just the smallest thing the Doctor said or did or some comment from the King of the Daleks or whatever he was. He had a good brain like that, if you were impressed by those sorts of things. He could see meaning in things others wouldn't even notice.

It was then, as we were walking past St. Mary Butts Church, heading towards town, that it suddenly occurred to me. Perhaps the one person who could help me understand what was happening to me had been under my nose all the time- Ash. But could I really tell him what I'd seen? What if he thought I was a crazy person or something? What if he told everyone at school, I'd never live it down. Worse still, what if he told my Mum? She'd have me locked up in Prospect Park for sure. That'd suit her down to the ground. She'd be able to move the plonker into our house. Or maybe even she'd move into his swanky place in Pangbourne and by the time I got released the house would be sold and I'd be homeless. Or at least I'd have to live with Gran. I loved her but she'd drive me mad if I had to live with her all the time. But still, Ash might just be able to help. I felt pretty sure if I could get him to promise not to tell anyone that he'd keep his word. He was all 'honourable' and shit when it came to stuff like that, felt that if you promised to do something then you should do it, whatever it cost you. And he believed in science fiction like it was fact so maybe he'd not find it so far-fetched to listen to me, to help me understand the meaning of what I'd seen.

And maybe he'd even be able to give other explanations Medusa hadn't even considered which would help make sense of it.

'Listen, it's a nice evening and we've been stuck in classes and the library all day, so why don't we walk back to your place instead of getting the bus- do us good. Your Mum won't be making dinner for ages yet, will she?'

'S'ppose not, if you want to,' he answered although I could see he was really cold, his nose was dripping and he had his scarf muffled right around his neck, his woolly hat with the ear flaps pulled down so he looked like a Bassett hound or something, with his big brown eyes looking out from under it.

And then it occurred to me, we should go to Forbury Gardens, go back to see the Maiwand Lion. Despite thinking about it all this time, I had not actually been back. I think I was a little scared or something, don't know if it was more about nothing happening than something happening again. But now, with Ash with me, I felt that it was the perfect time, and maybe the perfect place to tell him.

We walked down Broad Street. All the shops were lit up, Christmas lights blinking in their windows, fake presents gift-wrapped under fake Christmas trees, baubles big and small dangling and glistening under the lights, Santa Claus winking disconcertingly from *John Lewis*- always gave me the creeps even as a kid. There was a real buzz about the place, lots of people now well into their shopping, women mainly, lists clutched in their gloved hands, organising the perfect day for their families, buying something special for their kids and husbands or boyfriends. It occurred to me for a moment that my Mum might be among the shoppers. But I pushed the thought to the back of my mind.

Ash was still banging on about something about the Daleks when we had cut down behind M&S and were now approaching the Old Town Hall.

'Let's go through the graveyard behind St. Laurence's,' I said, striding forward, cutting Ash off mid-flow. I didn't wait for his reaction, just made for the alley between the old church and Blandy's, the solicitors' office. It was a short-cut we often took. When you're a geek, you need to know all the back ways and nooks and crannies in case you need to make a quick getaway from assholes you might bump into in town.

It was suddenly dark and quiet as we entered this hidden corner of town. There was stillness here. The ice on the footpath between the old Victorian headstones crunched under our feet as we walked. The grass around the graves was covered in frost as the sun had never penetrated the dark shadows cast by the church and the trees. Some people might think this was spooky but I thought it was beautiful. And diagonally opposite was Forbury Gardens, and the immense mass of the Maiwand Lion. I could feel it pull at me like a magnet. We jumped down the few small steps as we left the graveyard and now were only separated from the park by a narrow strip of road. A bus went trundling along, lit up, bright and busy, the driver taking his time on the bend as he drove by us.

'Let's cut through the park,' I said. 'We can cross the road on the other side by those lights by the other gate near the prison.' But I knew I wouldn't be rushing through the park. We entered up a couple of steps through the small side gate in the red-brick wall which surrounded the park onto the gravel footpath which traversed it and suddenly revealed, a dark mass against the lights of the office building surrounding, high on its plinth, the Maiwand Lion. The sight of it took my breath away and I stopped short. Ash crashed into me from behind.

'What are you doing?' he complained.

'Look, can we sit down for a second, I don't feel too good?'

'What, here? What's wrong with you? Are you going to throw up or something?' Ash didn't know whether to approach me to check on me or stand well back to avoid me hurling on him.

'No, nothing like that. I just feel a bit dizzy, is all. I just need to sit down for a few minutes, OK? There's a bench there, that'll do.'

'But it's covered in frost,' Ash whined.

'Well, sit on your bloody school bag, then!'

'OK, I was just saying, don't want to get piles or nothing '. He put his satchel on the bench like a dowager arranging a cushion on a seat at the opera and perched uncomfortably on it. I just folded the bottom half of my overcoat under my arse and sat down on it as best I could. But he was right, it was bloody freezing and I could feel the frost penetrate the back of my legs where they touched the bench. I leaned forward and let my head rest in my hands, looking down at the frozen gravel path for a second, inhaling and exhaling loudly a couple of times.

'Are you OK?' Ash's voice quiet now, concerned. I could feel his arm floating uselessly in the air, not sure whether to rest it on my shoulder or pat me on the back or what.

'Not really, Ash.' I sighed, still looking at the ground. 'Haven't been for a long-time, if I'm honest.'

Ash didn't answer but he did place his hand on my shoulder after all and patted it gently.

'Look, I've been trying to think of how to tell you this or even whether to tell you this for a while now.'

'Oh?' I could feel Ash gulp.

'No, don't worry,' I laughed dryly. 'I'm not coming out to you or anything!' Ash laughed too, protesting weakly that he didn't think that's what I meant but I could tell it probably was.

'It'd be a lot easier if it was something like that, mate, I promise you!' I laughed again. He laughed too, probably not realising why but not knowing what else to do.

'Look, I might as well just say it, what happened, I mean. But you've got to promise not to tell anyone, not even my mother, not even your Mum- promise?' I asked urgently.

'Yeah, OK, I promise. Look, you're scaring me now, Andrew. For god's sake, just spit it out will you. What the hell is it?'

I looked down at the ground again. It made it easier not to look at his face or to look up to where the Lion stood, looking down at me. I took a deep breath, and then started:

'Remember on Remembrance Sunday, when I was taken ill at the ceremony?'

'Of course, yeah' Ash answered, perplexed.

'Well, you know everyone thought I had some sort of seizure or something, when I collapsed?'

'Yeah, well you did, I saw you, remember? We were all there. You had a proper fit and everything, shaking, eyes rolling and stuff.'

'Thanks for that,' I answered sarcastically. 'Anyway, whatever you saw, I didn't have an epileptic seizure or whatever.'

'Well, I know you said the doctors couldn't find any signs of epilepsy when they examined you, but that doesn't mean it couldn't have happened as a once off thing, y'know. Maybe how you're feeling now is an aura, or something. I read up on it on Wikipedia. Oh, wait, maybe I should call someone or go and get help. Do you think you're going to have another one now?' I could hear the panic rising in Ash's voice.

'No, mate, don't worry, I'm fine, I'm not going to throw another wobbly. No, listen. What I mean is, that on that morning, whatever it was people saw happen to me, well, that was only the end of something, something which happened to me that morning, something I saw.'

'I don't understand what you mean, Andrew?' I could hear Ash's voice

73

sounded stressed. 'What are you going on about, mate?'

'The Lion, I'm going on about the Lion!' I looked up and pointed over to the Lion, standing there in the dark, looking down at us. Ash's face was full of confusion, he looked slowly from my face to the Lion, then back to me.

'I saw it move, Ash. That morning, at the ceremony. It moved. I couldn't believe what I was seeing. I mean, I know it sounds crazy, and clearly no one else saw it, but I did. It moved, it turned its head towards me, and it...it roared, y'know, proper roared, like the MGM lion at the start of the movies. I thought it was going to leap from the plinth and run amok. It was really fierce-looking, y'know. Proper angry. And the noise of that roar, it was so strong, mate, it went right through me, y'know. I could feel it here, in my chest or something, vibrating. It made me lose my breath, like my heart skipped beats or something, and that's when I went down, it made me light-headed and I collapsed!'

I stopped talking. I could see Ash's face, wide-eyed, just staring at me, disbelief writ large across his mug.

'You don't believe me! I should've known. No one believes me, but it's what happened, I swear. I swear on my father's grave, it's true!'

'I do believe you, Andrew,' Ash answered, quietly. I looked into his face. I couldn't help it, I sort of laughed, maybe it was relief, to have finally said it and have someone say they believe me.

'Really? You really believe me?'

'Yeah, of course. If you say you saw something then you saw something. Why would you say something like that unless it's what you believed? If you say you saw the lion move then I believe you think you saw it move.'

'No, wait,' I came back. 'I don't "think" I saw it move, I did see it move. It fucking roared and everything. It was staring right at me, y'know.'

Ash looked over at the mass of metal sitting on top of the plinth, like he was trying to believe me but having a hard time doing so.

'Well, it is really life-like, isn't it? I mean, I could imagine that if you were looking at it for a while then you might .....'

'Look!' I cut in. 'I'm not asking you to imagine anything. I'm asking you, as a friend, just to believe me, just accept what I'm saying to you, even if it does sound crazy or physically impossible. I mean, you bang on about *Star Trek* and *Doctor Who* and all that shit as if it is real, and then I tell you something, something amazing, something that happened here, to me, and the first thing you say is that I must have imagined it!'

Ash looked hurt. He looked down at his hands, now resting in his lap like a vicar taking confession. I could tell he was embarrassed. But then he seemed to rally, looked up and said:

'I'm sorry, Andrew. You're right. I should accept what you say, even if I don't understand it. I can't say that I comprehend how such a thing could happen but I do believe what you've said, I believe you saw it.'

'Really? You're not just saying this to humour me or shut me up?'

Ash shook his head solemnly.

'Thanks mate. That's all I'm asking you, to suspend your disbelief, just for a while. Just allow me that, for now.' Ash nodded again, more vigorously this time. I got up from the bench, my arse was frozen by then, and started to walk towards the Maiwand Lion, half-expecting him to roar again, half-hoping he would so then Ash could see for himself. But then, half of Reading was at the Remembrance Sunday service that morning and I was the only one to see what happened, as far as I knew anyway. Ash followed behind me, and then we both stopped and looked up at the Lion. The names of men killed in the Afghan 'campaign' were listed, metal letters on sheets of copper or bronze or whatever, verdigrised with age.

'It was so real, mate,' I said, breaking the silence which had dropped down between us like a mist. 'I haven't been back here since that morning, y'know. Probably afraid of a repeat performance.' Ash said nothing but just listened.

'It's been going round and round in my head, y'know, what does it mean? Why did I see it? Why then? Why here, y'know?' I looked at Ash. His face was lifted up towards the lion, like it had been that morning, Remembrance Sunday.

'So you think it's some sort of message? Some sort of sign?' he asked slowly, carefully, tasting each word in his mouth before uttering it.

'I don't know, maybe. But why not? *"There are more things in heaven and earth than are dreamt of in your philosophies, Horatio"*, that's what Hamlet said, isn't it? Maybe, just maybe, I'm not losing my mind; just maybe this means something, is that possible? Is there enough room in that multi-verse of yours for such things, eh?'

Ash shrugged. 'I don't know, mate, but maybe there is. Maybe this thing has connected you with something, in yourself if nowhere else. It is a war memorial, y'know, for the Afghan war, even if it is a hundred years or more ago. Perhaps it just brought something out of you, that...'

'You sound like my fucking shrink!' I could feel myself getting frustrated, angry. 'Look, I've heard all the Freudian bollocks and I simply don't accept it. I have had every corner of my brain probed and scanned. I even thought maybe I had a brain tumour, but all the time they fail to find something, something real to explain what I've seen, something I can believe in, anyway. So I'm left with this: what if it is a message or a sign? Maybe instead of trying to understand how I've seen what I've seen, I should be thinking about what it meant? You know, Hamlet doesn't get hung up on whether he's seen his father's ghost, he accepts it as real and then gets hung up on what he's meant to do about what it's told him.'

'But you're not Hamlet, and that's just a play,' Ash reasoned.

'I know, I'm not fucking mad or something. I'm just saying maybe in those days people knew how to interpret things like this better than we do, that maybe we've lost that ability, and we try to reason everything away instead of just accepting it, on face value. And maybe I should be thinking what this vision I had, or whatever it was, was actually trying to communicate to me. Maybe that's what I should be doing. And if it is, then I can't think of anyone better to help me than you. Will you, will you help me, Ash?'

Ash looked at me straight in the eye and said as if I even needed to ask. I felt relieved, accepted. Somehow, I felt, I'd moved forward. And then, from the sky, falling slowly, lazily, fluttering like white-winged moths, snowflakes, fat and soft. Ash looked skywards, and in an instant his glasses were splattered with snowflakes so big he had to remove them to see.

I looked up too and saw the head of the Maiwand Lion surrounded by a halo of snowflakes flurrying around his mane.

'We'd better go, Andrew, before this gets too heavy! If we run we can catch the bus from the station at a quarter past.'

And so we left, hurriedly, the snow falling around us, covering everything in white, quickly settling on the frozen ground, obscuring our footprints as they led away from the Maiwand Lion.

CHAPTER SEVEN

Annunciation

By the time I got home that evening it was pretty late. There had been a good covering of snow and it brought with it that sort of hushed tone you get as if everything is muffled under cotton-wool. Ash's Dad dropped me back. I liked him. He was a proper Dad, serious but funny; he told really lame jokes but you could tell he took life seriously. He was quite religious, something important down at the mosque but he wasn't one of those people who banged on about religion, you just sort of knew he was 'spiritual'. I often thought he would get on well with Gran even though in some ways they were opposite ends of a spectrum. But they both believed God involved Himself in their daily lives and concerns. I had no such belief, even then after I had started to think the Lion was some sort of apparition.

When I came through the door, I pulled my shoes off and was taking my coat off when Mum appeared. She looked serious. I was still in a mood with her so I had planned just to slip up stairs without saying anything to her but she'd caught me now before I'd been able to get away.

'Andrew, I'm glad you're back, I need to talk to you about something.'

I rolled my eyes 'cos I thought she was going to have another go at me about how she was entitled to have male friends and all that blah, blah, blah she came out with whenever I threw a strop about the plonker. So I tried to fob her off with saying how tired I was and all and that I just wanted to go to bed.

'I'm sorry, Andrew but this won't wait and I need to talk to you about it tonight. Look, come into the sitting room and sit down, so we can talk properly.' Reluctantly, I harrumphed my way through, sort of barging past her and flopped down onto the sofa in my usual spot. The TV was on but on mute. The BBC news showing some footage from Afghanistan, soldiers on patrol, crawling along at a snail's pace in some trench or something, probably worried about IEDs. Mum switched the telly off and sat down on the armchair so she was facing me.

'Look, Andrew, I know you've been a bit off with me recently and I think I know why but really, there's no need to behave like this towards me. No matter what, I'm still you're mother, and I love you, even if I don't always like you.' She tried a weak smile- this was a well-worn phrase in our house. I didn't respond, just looked at the blank TV screen, which now reflected me sitting slumped on the sofa and Mum perched tensely on the edge of the armchair.

'There's something I need to talk to you about but I'm a bit scared to do so because I don't know how you're going to feel about it...'

'Look, if it's about you and that plonker, Jonathan...'

She snapped that no, it wasn't about him at all, and then, almost as an afterthought, not to refer to him as 'the plonker' but I could see she was secretly amused by the way the corner of her lips twitched. But then she composed herself and started again, talking quietly and seriously.

'Andrew, I had a phone call today from a man who worked with your father, another soldier, who was with him in Afghanistan.' I was suddenly interested and a little bit scared because I suspected she was going to say something hard to hear.

'He was with your father when.....when he was...'

'Killed?' I cut in, impatiently, a bit angrily.

'He was there with him, helping him. He seems like a very nice man. His name is Sgt. Pearse. He worked with your Dad a long time, he said, knew him very well. He said how sorry he was that they could not save him.' Her voice faded out.

'Why did he call? What does he want?'

'Well, he wondered if it would help us, or you, to meet with him? He's home for Christmas, on leave. He's got family in London he's staying with. But he said he would really like to meet with us, with you. That it was what they promised each other, your Dad and him, that if one of them, well, y'know, they'd make sure their families were OK. He said he could come up and see us this week-end, Saturday, if you wanted to meet him. But he said it was up to you. He would completely understand if you didn't want to see him but he hoped you would. He has something to tell you, about your Dad and a few bits and pieces of his he thought you might want to keep. He's brought them back personally because he didn't want to risk them getting lost by the Army.'

I could feel myself getting choked up. I could feel my voice catch as I tried to answer.

'Yeah, I think I would like to meet him. I would, I think.' I couldn't say anything else just then. Mum said she'd call him back tomorrow and let him know and make arrangements. She said we should do it at home here, it would be more 'private'. I knew she meant she didn't want to risk me having another public meltdown if we met somewhere in town but I agreed with her.

'OK,' I said. 'I'm going to bed now, if that's alright. I feel really tired.'

'Do you want Uncle Edward or Gran to be here as well, on Saturday, I mean. For moral support, maybe?'

'Maybe. I'll think about it.' I got up and made for the door. 'Thanks, Mum,' I said. She smiled, warmly this time. I could see there were some tears brimming in her eyes. There were in mine too, probably.

That night I slept badly. Between telling Ash about the Lion and then hearing that this mate of Dad's wanted to see me, I could hardly switch my brain off. I probably nodded off somewhere before three AM so when it came time to get up for school, I was in no mood to get out of my bed. It had snowed through the night and there was a build-up on the roads and footpaths which hushed the traffic. Mum had porridge ready for me when I got up. I sat down and poured honey over it, glad of the warmth as it slid down my throat. It wasn't bad either. Maybe she'd been practicing or getting tips from Gran.

'You OK, Andrew,' she asked, putting her hand on my forehead, which I shrugged away. 'You look terrible, did you not sleep so well last night?' I grunted that I hadn't but I'd be fine once I'd eaten.

'I thought maybe they'd close the school with the snow and everything but the council have been out gritting the roads all night so apparently everything's moving OK.'

I didn't respond. The voice on the radio, BBC Berkshire, spoke of further British losses in Afghanistan, two soldiers killed by IEDs yesterday, one was 21 years old and the other a man in his forties with two kids.

'Poor children,' my mother sighed almost to herself. 'These things always seem worse this close to Christmas.' I didn't say anything. Seemed to me it was much the same when you lost your father, whether it was Christmas, Easter or the August Bank Holiday week-end. But I sort of knew what she meant. We ate in silence, her crunching her toast noisily in her usual way, crumbs going everywhere. 'Mum, you've got crumbs down your front, as usual!'

'Oops,' she giggled, wiping them away with the bit of kitchen roll she was using as a napkin. 'I'm always doing that!' For a moment, I could see the girl she used to be in her face.

'Gosh, look at the time, I'll be late,' she said, rushing over to the sink to deposit her unwashed cup in the washing-up basin. 'I'll do those when I get in this evening.' She always said that, some way to assuage her guilt that she was being slovenly by leaving stuff in the sink instead of washing it up straight away. Gran would never do that. She wouldn't leave the house unless everything was 'just so' because 'you never know the day or the hour and I wouldn't want anyone coming back to the house to say I didn't keep the place clean!' she'd say every single time. Always the optimist, my Gran. Still, I have to admit, it was much nicer coming back to a clean and tidy house than one like ours with everything piled up in the dish and the marmalade pots and stuff still on the breakfast table. I suppose I should really tidy them away myself but I couldn't be arsed.

'What time's your bus?' Mum asked, in a flurry of coat, scarf and handbag as she rushed to get ready to leave.

'Same as it always is, if it turns up,' I answered.

'Keys, keys, where are the bloody...oh, there they are....'

'Exactly where the always are,' I finished her sentence for her.

'Right, well, I'm off, then,' she said, and suddenly rushed forward, hugged me, kissed me on the cheek, leaving a lipstick smudge which I urghhed at and wiped off. 'I love you, you know that don't you?'

'Yeah, yes, I know.' I could tell she was feeling bad for me because of what she told me about last night. She's like that, sort of over-compensates for bad things by getting all emotional. She gets that from Gran, too. Still, it was nice to know she cared although I knew she did really. I hugged her back. I could smell that perfume I'd gotten her for her birthday which she wore all the time now even though I think she didn't like it that much.

At school later that day we had a free study period so Ash and I took up our usual position in the library. Natasha wasn't at school that day, off sick or something. We had a couple of end of term exams to study for next week, English and History. I wasn't too worried, although this term my grades hadn't been as good as usual, they weren't too bad either and I knew I'd get by well enough and they didn't really matter too much anyway.

It was unusual for Ash to appear distracted during study period but he spent a lot of time staring out the window instead of reading his book. There were only a few others in the library and when the guy on our table left, Ash whispered:

'Andrew, I've been thinking about what you told me last night, about the lion.'

'Ssssh!' I hissed, looking round urgently for eaves-droppers.

'It's fine, there's no one can hear us if we whisper.' I could smell faint traces of cardamom on his breath. I agreed we could whisper when I realised no one was now on our table.

'I've been doing some research on-line, spent ages on it last night after you'd gone home, got told off by my Dad actually when he saw the light was still on in my bedroom after midnight when he got up to pee, which he does a lot now, something to do with his prostate, Mum says, but he won't see...'

'Ash!' I cut in. 'Can we move on from the subject of your Dad's waterworks, please! Did you find anything out about the Lion?'

'Well, there's loads of stuff about it and the Battle of Maiwand, really interesting, actually. But that wasn't what I was researching. I was thinking more about what you said about what you saw and what happened to you. I wanted to see if I could come up with anything that might explain it or at least help us understand what it was you saw.'

'You mean apart from me having a brain tumour or going mad, or both?' Ash wrinkled his nose and pushed his specs up like he always does when he's not sure if someone is making a joke or not.

'Well, actually, they were the most obvious reasons I could find to explain what you experienced.' He said this without a trace of sarcasm.

'Well, let's assume, for the sake of argument, that it's neither of those things.' I left him no room for doubt that I was being sarcastic.

'OK. Then you could be making it all up, of course.'

'Oh, thanks very much. You think I'm some attention seeker now!' I could hear the anger in my own voice. 'Well, if I was just saying these things so people would make a fuss of me or something, then why have I told no one but you?'

'No, I know, I know,' Ash quickly reassured. 'I'm just listing all the possibilities, you know, like Sherlock Holmes!' He smiled. '"*When you have excluded all that is possible, whatever remains, however improbable, must be true*".' I recognised the quote, one of Ash's favourite.

'OK, Sherlock, so what have you deduced, then?'

'Well, I don't know really. Just that whatever you saw is not easily explained, not if we accept the laws of physics as we understand them.'

'You mean, it's a bit like UFOs or the Bermuda Triangle or something?' I scoffed.

'Well, not really. There is usually something which could explain unusual lights in the sky or ships or planes disappearing. No, this is more 'supernatural' than that.'

'Supernatural? What like ghosts and ghouls and things that go bump in the night?'

Ash didn't rise to the bait. 'No, supernatural, as in beyond nature. Whatever you saw cannot be explained by our understanding of the laws of nature, so we have to think beyond the norms.'

'I don't think I understand you, Ash. Are you taking the mickey or something?'

'No, no, really. If you go on-line and try to find things that look or sound similar to what you've described, you keep getting pointed to religious texts. You know, apparitions, burning bushes, angels appearing, that sort of thing. It's the only type of category I can find into which to place what you experienced!'

The last few words hung in the air between us. Ash, with his deadly logic and rigorous approach had essentially reached the same conclusion I had independently. I giggled a bit, whether from relief or feeling ridiculous, I don't really know. But there it was, we were in the realm of weeping statues and Our Lady of Lourdes again.

'So, I've had some sort of religious experience, then?' I asked slowly, half-sarcastically. 'But I don't even have much of a religious faith, not really. And the Maiwand Lion is hardly a religious icon or whatever, is it?'

'No, it's not about being religious, it's about the meaning you ascribe to the thing you're seeing. The Maiwand Lion has a meaning to you, maybe. It represents something for you.'

I was about to come back with some response but my tongue caught and I found I couldn't speak for a few seconds. So the moment hung there between us. I could see Ash's eyes scanning my face from behind his *SpecSavers* specs, trying to figure out if I was figuring out what he had already concluded. But when I didn't respond, he helped me out, like we were doing a maths problem:

'It's the war. The war in Afghanistan. Don't you see it? The Maiwand Lion is a war memorial from the last time the British Army lost men in Afghanistan. You lost your Dad in the war in Afghanistan recently.' He paused, letting me catch-up with him, but I remained sitting there with my mouth open like I was brain-damaged or something, and maybe I was.

'The lion represents a potent symbol of loss for you, Andrew. It is a very real presence connecting you and your loss to the lives of people from over a century ago from this place who suffered the same loss as you have, in the same place, almost literally in the same place. Perhaps this was something your unconscious mind latched onto and created a 'vision' for you at the Remembrance Sunday wreath-laying ceremony?'

'So, we're back to me losing my marbles, then?' I found my voice again when the conversation moved onto the same territory Medusa had touched upon.

'No, not at all. It's not about you losing the plot, it's about your brain being stimulated in a specific way that made you have a 'religious' experience.' My face obviously told Ash I wasn't buying into his explanation but before I could get a word in he pushed on.

'Neuroscientists have been studying brain functions for a while now to try to find what they call the "God Spot", you know, the collection of neurons that fire up when people have what they perceive to be a 'religious experience'. Even the Dalai Lama supports the work. He thinks it will help people to understand that spirituality is as fundamental a part of human existence and behaviour as anything else which defines us as human: emotions, fear, hunger, love, sexuality, all that stuff.'

'But isn't that just another way to say people are deluded if they believe in all this stuff, that it's just a random bunch of neurons firing in response to a stimulus. That religion could be 'cured' if we cut out the area of the brain involved or gave people drugs, like an 'anti-Catholic pill' or something?' I chuckled at my own joke. But Ash remained serious, even looking a bit pissed off that I didn't seem to get what he was driving at.

'Well, they'd have a job cutting the areas out of the brain without killing us! That's the point, Andrew- these parts of the brain the researchers have identified are so integral to us, so fundamental, that we couldn't survive without them. And think about it, they've been preserved, maybe even developed, through thousands of years of evolution. So they must serve some purpose. And maybe they're there to help us understand the world we live in, even to appreciate it in a way beyond just what our senses can perceive in the normal way.'

'Maybe those areas of the brain created God,' I cut in. 'Maybe religion is only the workings of our imagination.'

'Maybe, but even if it is, it seems somehow necessary for us, something we need. Even atheists and non-believers have these responses to various stimuli. Which gets me back to the point I was trying to make to you: it doesn't matter whether you believe in God or Santa Claus, these areas light up like a Christmas tree in response to stimuli to which we attribute "spiritual significance". So we literally create God in our own image because we determine the nature of the divine, or at least our brain does. So when we see or hear or feel something that has a particular meaning for us, well then these parts of the brain respond, we 'feel' as if we're in the presence of God or having some religious apparition...'

'Like seeing a solid iron lion move,' I said, slowly trying to comprehend what Ash was saying.

'Maybe,' he answered quietly, like he did when I got the answer to maths problems he helped me with even if I didn't understand exactly how I'd done it. 'But because our brain has a particular understanding of the environment we live in, because it tries to rationalise what we're seeing, when it perceives something which simply isn't logical, it tries to make sense of it using other points of reference, like maybe the feelings you had when you looked at the lion that morning would only make sense to the logical part of your brain if the lion had done something extraordinary....'

'Like move,' I cut in, barely audible, even to myself.

'Maybe,' Ash answered satisfied I finally got what he was saying, QED. We remained silent for a minute or so after that, mulling over everything Ash had said, turning it over like we were examining a gemstone, looking for flaws. Finally, I spoke.

'There's only one thing left I don't understand?'

'Oh?' Ash, like an owl hooting.

'Why are we paying Dr. Medusa when you've figured it out so beautifully?' Ash scanned my face for a second before realising it was a joke, and then we both laughed. Although, I wasn't joking!

When I got home that evening after school, Uncle Edward was there. He was sitting at the kitchen table huddled together with Mum over a cafetiére drained to the dregs. This could only mean that they'd had a two cup conversation which could only mean that I had been the subject of their discussions. They played it all non-chalant when I came in, greeting me warmly, asking about my day at school and all that. Mum asked me if I wanted a hot drink, saying she could pop the kettle on. I nahed her and grabbed a carton of *Tropicana* from the fridge but before I could slurp from it she yelled 'use a glass.' I could see Uncle Edward smile to himself at this obvious piece of well-rehearsed interplay between us both.

'Why don't you sit down with us while you drink your OJ, Andrew?' Uncle Edward retained some Americanisms in his speech from his time working in the States when he was younger. I pulled up the chair beside him. I didn't mind, I liked Uncle Edward.

'Your Mum tells me you're expecting a visitor on Saturday?'

So this was it, the reason for the friendly chat. I nodded, like it was no big deal.

'Are you sure you want to meet this chap, Andrew? You mustn't feel that you have to if you don't want to.'

'No, I do, really. I've been thinking about it all day. I know it might be upsetting but Dad asked this guy to meet his family if, y'know, anything bad happened to him. So it's like doing what he asked, or something. Seems bad form not to meet him, especially if he's giving up time with his own family to come and see me.'

Uncle Edward smiled, satisfied no doubt that I'd thought about it seriously. 'That's very mature of you, Andrew. I have to admit to being a bit concerned that this might prove too much for you after recent events,' he paused, awkward, aware he'd mentioned the taboo subject. 'But it might help you get ...'

'Don't say closure, please! You sound like Medusa when you say things like that!'

'Medusa?'

'Dr. Markiewicz, the shrink lady.' I could see his disapproval even as he oohed in recognition. He didn't approve of people slagging off professionals, even one's he didn't necessarily rate.

'Well, Andrew, I'm sure she's very competent so if she thought such things were important for you then she's possibly correct even if you don't see it.' He paused then moved on to the real reason for his visit. 'Speaking of Dr. Markiewicz, she is available should you need to see her after tomorrow's meeting, even this close to Christmas, she's happy to arrange an appointment for you if you want one?'

'No doubt, she could do with some extra cash to finish off her Christmas shopping!'

'Andrew!' Mum snapped at me, reminding me of my manners. 'There's no need to be like that. Your uncle is just trying to help you and Dr. Markiewicz is also there to help you. There's no need to be rude. I'm sorry, Edward, I think this is a difficult time for Andrew. I'm sure he will apologise to you for being so cheeky.'

Her eyes burned with reprimand at me.

'Look, I don't need some shrink to help with cope with things,' I said sarcastically as I could summon. 'I'm sorry if my making my own choices or comments appears rude to anyone but it is my choice, and I don't appreciate being pressurised into agreeing to see someone I don't think I need to see.'

Uncle Edward blushed a little with emotion, flustering that he hadn't meant to pressurise me into anything but was trying to ensure I had help dealing with difficult things if I needed it, that was all. But he was sorry if I had taken it differently. I was blushing now, it was so unusual for me to have even a cross-word with Uncle Edward. But I felt like they were manoeuvring me into agreeing to something I didn't want to do even if they were motivated by a desire to help me. Medusa knew too much and had coaxed me into saying things I didn't mean to tell her. I worried that she would end up recommending that I was sectioned or something and I didn't want to deal with that. Why couldn't they all be like Ash? Why couldn't they just listen and try to understand? Why did their so-called help feel so much like an attack?

I got up from the table, saying I had some homework to finish. As I reached the door, I turned and said to Mum: 'About what you asked last night, I'd prefer to see Sgt. Pearse alone tomorrow. I don't need anyone else to hold my hand. I'm all grown-up now, in case people hadn't noticed. This visit is to speak to me, no one else.'

I could see my words hit home on Mum's face which registered a mixture of anger and affront. She looked at Uncle Edward, who was sitting with his back to me now. I could see she was about to rise from her chair, no doubt to challenge me but Uncle Edward reached and touched her forearm, shaking his head slightly and she looked in his face and sat down again, fiddling with the teaspoon in her saucer like she always did when she was biting her tongue but fit to burst.

That night, Friday night, I didn't come back down stairs. I sat in my bedroom, exchanging e-mails with Ash, looking up some of the stuff he'd told me about on the internet and checking out my friends on Facebook. Natasha's said she'd been feeling ill for days now, that she was seeing the doctor the next day, putting in one of those frowny sad emoticons at the end of her comment. I pinged her that I hoped she would feel better soon but she didn't reply, probably 'cos it was so late and if she was sick she'd probably gone to bed. I could hear Mum pottering about downstairs all evening. She'd shouted up if I wanted anything special for dinner, an Indian take-away or something, but I told her no, even though I did fancy it. She knocked on my bedroom door a while later, saying she'd brought me up a tray. I grunted that I was busy so she said she'd leave it outside and I could pick it up when I was ready. I could smell the food wafting under the door and I did feel hungry so I opened it up and found a tray containing a plate of curry and rice from the Indian down the road, with some onion bhajees and nann bread and a glass of coke with ice so I took it in and ate it at my desk. It was slightly colder than I'd preferred but I enjoyed it anyway. I did feel a bit bad about not coming down to eat with my mother and imagined her sitting downstairs with a tray on her lap watching the telly but I couldn't get beyond my annoyance with her so stayed where I was.

A while later, I could hear her on the phone, talking in tones that suggested she was annoyed and upset. No doubt she'd phoned the plonker to cry on his shoulder. I could hear her say my name occasionally, and then my Dad's name! Made my blood boil! What was she doing discussing Dad with the plonker! It never really occurred to me that she might talk about this sort of stuff with him, not really. I suppose I didn't really think about her needing to talk to anyone about things, well, maybe Gran and Uncle Edward, but not anyone else. And why would she want to talk to her 'boyfriend' about her dead ex-husband anyway? No doubt slagging him off and saying she was glad to see the back of him so she could 'move on with her life'! She could be such a cold bitch at times, thinking only of herself. Then I heard her voice change, more broken, sounded like she was crying, talking to him and crying. Made me feel bad then, that I'd thought those thoughts about her. But I wouldn't let this persuade me to go downstairs to see if she was alright.

About an hour later, I heard her come up stairs, pausing outside my door. I thought she was going to knock, to speak with me or something but she never did, just stood there for a few seconds then went on to her own bedroom. I switched off the computer and TV and i-pod and climbed into bed. I was exhausted having not slept well the night before but still upset and anxious about what had happened that day and would happen tomorrow. I realised then I didn't even know what time tomorrow the guy was arriving but figured it wouldn't be before mid-morning at the earliest as he was coming up from London. I set my alarm clock for eight AM then lay there, staring at the ceiling before eventually falling into a dreamless and heavy sleep.

CHAPTER 8

Visitation

That Saturday morning I woke up feeling really nervous, like I was going to take a really hard, really important exam or something. I hadn't expected to feel this way. I suppose I'd trivialised the visit with the mate of my dead Dad just to avoid bottlin' out of seeing him. Even Ash thought it might be a difficult thing to do when I chatted with him on-line the night before, especially given 'how I'd been feeling lately.' But I thought despite my apprehension that it was an important thing for me to do and something my Dad would have expected me to do. Besides, I hadn't just been saying it for effect the night before when I'd said that this guy was giving up precious time with his own family to come to visit me so that had to count for something. Still, I did kind of wish he'd phone to say he couldn't make it. Mum appeared beside me in the kitchen, red-eyed, in her dressing gown, clearly having slept little the night before. She had a coffee cup in her hand, drained to the dregs, and was intending to have more. She wished me a good morning in a washed out voice, croaky from lack of sleep.

'Sgt. Pearse is coming here around two o'clock. He phoned last night when you were in your room. I thought to call you but then in the mood you were in yesterday decided against it.' I mumbled thanks for telling me and focussed on buttering the toast I was sorting out for breakfast. She continued:

'I had a nice chat with him, actually. He seems like a really decent man. He was very close to your father.'

So that's who she was talking to last night on the phone, not the plonker. I suddenly felt really bad. I had misunderstood what had been going on. She had been talking to this mate of Dad's about him, and me, not talking to the plonker at all.

'I'm sorry about yesterday,' I mumbled. 'I guess I felt like I was sort of ambushed by you and Uncle Edward when I came in from school. It caught me off guard. I didn't mean to upset anyone, especially before today.' I felt her hand on my shoulder and her coffee breath whispering in close to my face.

'I know it's hard, Andrew. But you're not the only one going through this, you know. And everyone wants to help you, even if sometimes they don't know how to and even if you feel you don't need help. It doesn't seem all that long ago I was teaching you how to tie your shoelaces. Now you don't seem to need me for anything at all. But I can't help how I feel. I can't help wanting to help you. I know this past few months have been the most difficult of your life; they have been for me too, even if you think I've just moved on. Once you love someone, have a child with them, they're a big part of your life forever, even if things don't work out as you would have wished. I don't know if you can understand this but I never stopped loving your father, I just couldn't continue to live with him. He was a man who seemed to be on a path to self-destruction and I was worried he was going to destroy us, too. You're a lot like him in some ways: stubborn, proud, too proud to even ask for help never mind accept it when it's offered. But I hope you also have the good sense to see things as they really are, eventually. When the anger subsides and you look around you, Andrew, you'll see me and all your family and friends here for you, willing to help you in any way they can, and I hope when that day comes you'll accept that help.'

I didn't respond, just listened. I felt both sad and happy to hear what she said, especially about her not stopping loving Dad. But I also knew she was telling the truth about him. Just before he went to Afghanistan last time, he seemed to be very sad and upset with himself and everyone else. He pushed people away, pushed me away. The drink didn't help. It brought out a nasty part of his character that frightened me, and Mum. And I knew Mum had just wanted to protect me and that it wasn't just in response to a single incident she'd left him but because for years now he'd been acting stranger and stranger. She once said to him that every time he came back from a tour of duty, he'd left something of himself back there, where he'd been fighting, and that we were getting the ghost of him, cold, remote and dead to feeling. I never will forget those words of hers. I wasn't meant to hear them of course but because they were rowing so loudly I'd woken up and listened, frightened and cowering on the landing. I should have been braver, intervened, so many chances but I was a coward and never did. Now there would never be another chance. But I didn't say anything to Mum, I just stood there, staring at my stupid toast, scraping butter over it again and again until I felt her hand fall away from my shoulder as she went to put the kettle on to make more coffee.

The remainder of the morning dragged in a drip drop of time slipping slowly by, each minute carving into me like a tattoo. Mum asked me again if I'd wanted to have either her or Uncle Edward or even Gran with me when I met Sgt. Pearse but I reiterated my intention to meet him alone even though I wanted to scream yes to her offer of support. I would rather anything other than meet him alone but pride prevented me from saying different. In the end, she said she'd stay to welcome him and then leave us to it. I agreed, secretly glad I didn't have to spend the hours before he came alone. I tried to fill the time with getting myself ready, showering, dressing, re-dressing as if going on date or something. By the time the hour of his arrival was approaching, Mum and I were both perched nervously on the sofa, lost in a quagmire of our own thoughts, wishing the time would pass quickly and yet dreading the moment he came. We both startled when the doorbell rang.

'That must be him,' Mum said anxiously, getting up then looking at me, her eyes wide with concern. 'Last chance, should I stay or go?'

'I'd prefer to see him alone, please. Just let him in and then make your excuses, will you, please?'

'OK, OK,' she hissed without attempting to hide her frustration. She went into the hall. I could hear her voice assume that tone she puts on when she's trying to be polite. I heard a man's voice, indistinct but clearly Northern Irish in accent. Suddenly, he was there, in the living room, filling the door space, not a big man but wide, broad shoulders. I don't know why exactly but I had half expected him to be in uniform. Of course, he was in civvies, jeans, a heavy leather jacket, and a scarf, tartan, somehow ridiculous, which he was unwrapping now as he came through. The only trace of the war on him was the deep tan which carved wrinkles around his eyes like a river through a desert canyon. His ginger hair shorn short against his brown skull gave his head a sort of amber halo. I had leapt to my feet nervously. He was all good humour and joviality. He almost leapt forward to offer his hand to me saying:

'And this must be the bauld Andrew? Sure, yer the spitting image of your Dad, God rest him. It's like looking at him, so it is. The eyes, exactly the same.' I could feel myself blushing. Mum was taking his jacket from him, and his scarf. 'Thanks, Missus,' he said, turning to her. 'Bit of a shock to the system, this weather, given where we've just come from, if you know what I mean?'

'I'm sure it must be, Sgt. Pearse. One of many things which must be strange for you. Please, sit down, make yourself comfortable. Can I get you a tea or coffee?'

'A coffee would be grand, thanks, especially if you could Irish it up for me, if y'know what I mean?' He winked at me conspiratorially, as if we were old mates. 'Keeps the cold out like nothin' else can.' I could see Mum looking confused for a second before realising that he meant to add some whiskey to it. I could see she was a bit taken aback, drinking at this time of the day, I knew she was thinking, but didn't like to say anything to offend her guest and keen to make him feel welcome, she agreed she'd get him something to warm him up and went off to find where she'd stashed the Irish Whiskey she'd bought in for Gran for Christmas (who was also partial to an Irish Coffee).

I was suddenly aware that I was alone with Sgt. Pearse. I felt awkward and tongue-tied. Didn't know quite what to say or do, whether to sit or stand, smile or frown but I needn't have worried as Sgt. Pearse was more than capable of keeping the conversation going all by himself. He was garrulous, funny and friendly. I could see why he'd be friends with Dad. I could imagine them swapping war stories over many a pint. He went on about how he'd only gotten back the other day but it already felt like he'd never been away, that it was probably a trick of the mind, to allow us to cope with difficulties, to sort of gloss over unpleasant things and focus on the here and now. I told him his family must be glad to see him back, safely (a bit too loaded, hadn't meant to make it sound that way but he either didn't notice the tone or chose to ignore it) and within seconds he had the wallet out, and the gappy-toothed grin of his seven-year old and slightly surly face of his ten year old and his plump wife were grinning at me from a photograph, all ginger too, the whole lot of them. Told me his wife was Scottish, like my Dad, hence all the 'ginger nuts'. I laughed nervously but glad he was able to make a joke of it. Mum arrived in at that moment, the steaming hot cup of coffee laced with whiskey proffered before her, eyes lighting on the photo, oohs and ahhs of adoration for the children, how proud he must be of them, him swelling with paternal pride, not hiding his love, me a bit jealous, Mum sidling up to the armchair's arm a bit too much, leaning in, looking at another photo of the ginger nuts together, when the littlest one was a baby, a christening photo, the wife slimmer but still fat, the sergeant red-faced and more red-headed than now, all beaming, a happy family. 'You must be very proud of them, Sgt. Pearse.'

'Paddy, please, I've told you.'

'Patrick Pearse?' I blurted out, 'Is that your real name?' I couldn't believe that someone would be named after one of the leaders of the 1916 Rising in Dublin.

'Aye, hard to credit it, I know, but the Da was a real Republican, old school, mind you, not one of those cowardly bastards what blows up women and children out for a day's shoppin'. No better than the Taliban those Provo fuckers. Pardon the language, Katie!' He grinned like a naughty school boy who'd spoken out of turn with the teacher. He'd called her Katie. No one ever called her that. At least, not now. But that was the name Dad had called her, when they were together and relaxed with each other. Katie. That was what he must have called her when he spoke about her to his mate. She realised this too, glancing furtively over at me, perched familiarly yet nervously on the edge of the armchair holding family photos of her dead husband's friend. She blushed, only slightly, no one else would have noticed it, but I did.

Sgt. Pearse slurped appreciatively from his coffee mug, letting out a loud 'Aaaah! Grand wee drop, Katie. Irish, obviously!'

'Bushmills,' she answered, pleased with herself. It's Jamie's favourite.' We all suddenly realised she'd used the present tense when talking about my father. 'Even though he was Scottish, he preferred Irish whiskey.' She'd reverted to the past tense, she was floundering, gabbling, realising her mistake but trying to cover it up by talking more. 'My Mum always said that he only said that to ingratiate himself to her but I told her he didn't care if she liked him or not and that I was the only woman in this family who's good books he was keen to stay in!' She forced a slightly manic smile. I could see Sgt. Pearse had picked up on everything but he soldiered on with forced jollity.

'Aye, he mentioned yer Ma, right enough. Formidable woman, I'm told. And from the auld sod, too, I believe. That must be where you get yer good looks from, Andy, just like me- good genes!' He winked conspiratorially at me, but I was grateful that he moved us on from Mum's faux pas and her obvious attempt to cover it up. 'Any road, *sláinte*!' He gulped again from the cup having raised it in toast to me. I glared at Mum to signal to her to clear off. I knew she'd do this. She always wanted to be at the centre of things. She couldn't bear that Sgt. Pearse had come to see me, not her. It suited her to play the grieving widow sometimes. Not of course when the plonker was wooing her. She picked up on my dagger looks and told Sgt. Pearse she was going back to the kitchen to make a few sandwiches for lunch. He protested that she shouldn't go to any trouble on his behalf but she insisted and said that we two 'boys' probably had stuff to talk about in private, anyway. I was glad she left, she was so embarrassing.

'Yer Ma's a great woman, Andy, so she is. Must be a hard time for both of you, I'm sure.' I shrugged agreement, but wanted to move the subject away from my mother so I asked questions about how long he'd known Dad. He was glad of the opportunity to reminisce and expanded volubly on their shared history together. I heard about the various campaigns they'd been involved in, some stories about 'a few scrapes' they'd been in, all very told with real affection, conjuring up the presence of my father as if in the room, familiar, so much so I could almost smell him, perhaps because they both used the same aftershave. And yet the man I was hearing about from Paddy Pearse was not the one I'd known, at least not entirely. He was funny, loyal, brave, 'a real character'. His men loved him. They'd 'follow him into Hell and back, and sometimes they did.' He was great for keeping a smile on everyone's face, a real 'cod'. But he also took soldiering very seriously, a 'soldier's soldier'. He could come down on people like a ton of bricks if he thought they were slacking or lazy or not pulling their weight. Yet if he got what he wanted from someone, he'd love them like a brother and give you his last drop of blood if you'd ask him or even if you didn't. This man was the hero I had been told about by so many people so often that I had begun to wonder whether he'd really existed at all. But he was a different man with 'his men' and perhaps truly himself, more at home with them than he'd ever been with Mum and me. They'd respected and admired him. With us he was never quite what we'd wanted him to be, never quite good enough for Mum or at least that was what he thought, especially in the later years of their marriage. He perceived in her looks a derision, a sense that somehow he'd not lived up to her expectations, that their life together was not what she'd hoped for and less fancy than she should have deserved. She protested that she didn't feel like that at all but the truth was probably somewhere in the middle. The man we knew was often uncomfortable around us and seemed always to be wishing he was somewhere else. He didn't seem to really unwind when he was at home and appeared to us to look forward to getting back to 'his real family'. He didn't seem to need us as much as he needed them but maybe this had been an unfair assessment of his feelings. The man Paddy Pearse knew was someone to know, someone to be proud to know, and a devoted family man who never stopped talking about how proud he was of his beautiful wife and genius of a son, who would one day go on to become a doctor. Paddy told us they use to slag him off about his bragging, wondering how his wife ever walked again having given birth to a son with such a big brain his head must've been the size of a beach ball! Paddy Pearse laughed, winking at me like I was one of his mates, realising then he'd probably gone a bit far, the whiskey loosening his tongue. 'Begging yer pardon, young fella, no disrespect intended towards yer Ma.'

Just then Mum came in, with a huge plate of sandwiches, ham, chicken, cheese and pickle, like she was catering a buffet or something. Paddy's eyes lit up, and he roared in appreciation at the sight of this 'veritable feast, b' god! Sure you're a great woman! And another cup of coffee to wash these down would be much appreciated.' Mum smiled indulgently, pleased her generous hosting was appreciated and told him she'd warm another cup for him, her own accent drifting more towards Gran's than I was used to hearing, a drop of Irish whirling through it like cream through coffee.

When she returned, Paddy begged her to sit down on the couch, too. She looked at me for permission or something, but I was happy to smile yes, feeling I'd gotten as much as I was likely to from Dad's mate at this stage. But a few sandwiches in and well down his second mug of 'Irish coffee', he asked my Mum if she could fetch his jacket for him. 'Oh, you're not leaving already are you?' she asked, genuinely regretting it if he was. 'Not just yet, no missus, but I've just remembered that I got a few wee things in my pocket I need to pass onto young Andy before I forget.'

I looked at him then her as she left to go to the hall where she'd draped his heavy black leather jacket on the newel post of the stairs. She handed it over to him and he half got up to take it from her, muttering how hard it was to get up these days once he got settled, laughing at himself, and moaning about old age catching up on him.

He reached into his pocket, retrieving a padded brown envelope from within its quilted depths. He explained that he'd promised Dad to get these few wee bits and pieces to us if anything ever happened to him and not to trust it to the Army so he was fulfilling the promise by being here today. I leaned in, excited and fearful in equal measure, as if this man could somehow conjure up my father magically, half hoping and dreading this. He gently spilled the contents onto the coffee table in front of us. Service medals and their ribbons, in velvet boxes like the ones you got from the jewellers. He opened then up and told us about each one, explaining their significance, how they'd been won, what they meant to my father and to him, and he hoped, to me. I took each one as it was handed to me by my mother, with appropriate reverence, admiring them, their shiny faces representing whole periods of my father's life and achievements. He then presented us with some photographs, a little dog-eared and battered. One of him and my mother, on their wedding day, both much younger, almost unrecognisable; another, of him and Mum with me, as a baby, maybe at my christening. And then another final one, handed directly to me, with Sgt. Pearse saying how Dad always touched this one for luck before he ever went on patrol and whenever he returned safely. My eyes fell upon an image of Dad and me, smiling, in bright summer sunshine, taken a few years ago, in Forbury Park, in front of the Maiwand Lion. It caught me, like jumping into cold water, and made my heart skip a few beats. How could I have forgotten this? It all suddenly came back, that day, the picnic in Forbury Park, a hot July day, my birthday in fact, me and Dad, playing football, kicking it back and forwards together, among the people lying on blankets or just on the grass, enjoying the sunshine. Mum with us, wearing sunglasses, happy or so it seemed, setting things out on the tartan picnic blanket, treats from M&S, a summer dress, floral, but not as bright as the banks of flowers scattered around the green grass where we played. 'Let's get a photo,' Dad shouting playfully over to Mum, 'Me and Andy, together.' Us grinning together, kneeling down, me with one knee on the football, like I'd seen them do in the newspapers, Dad kneeling behind me, his hands on my shoulders, his voice in my right ear, 'Smile, Andy, one for the family album.' Mum, peering at us through the viewfinder of the camera. Click, the image captured forever. Dad and me, kneeling on the green, green grass of Forbury Park on a bright July day, in front of the Lion. How could I have forgotten this? It seemed a lifetime ago now, and so it was in many ways, at least his lifetime.

Sgt. Pearse could sense my intense focus on the photograph. He decided now was the time to tell me what he'd really wanted to tell me since he came through the front door. He asked me first. 'Do you want me to tell you how it happened, Andy?' Mum gasped slightly but audibly. She started forward. 'I don't think so, Paddy...' But I cut her off, with an emphatic yes, yes, I do want to know, please. Tell me, tell me what happened, really happened, not the sanitised version I've been given.

Paddy looked at my Mum. 'The boy's got a right to know, luv. Don't worry, I know what I'm doing, it's not the first time I've had to do this, unfortunately.' He leaned forward and looked me straight in the eye and said:

'Andy, your Da was one of the bravest men I ever knew. He was loved by his men and he loved them. Not any one of us wouldn't have stood in his place that morning but it was his turn, there's no way to avoid it when it's your turn. We'd been out for about an hour, following up on reported sightings of Taliban activists in the area. We suspected they'd been planting IEDs. We went along, very slowly, clearing the way as we went, destroying IEDs we came upon and we came upon loads. It was difficult work, and the heat, well, you can only imagine, even the hottest day of the year here wouldn't even approach it. And all the gear we have to carry, too. We were tired, hard work. Maybe we got sloppy, I don't know. But whatever happened, we were walking along this dried out river bed, a narrow channel really, not more than a few feet wide, you could nearly touch the sides with your hands if you stretched them out. And we were going along in single file, your Da out in front, as usual. Then a loud bang, the force of it nearly blew me off my feet. I was a couple of yards or more directly behind him. There was this terrific cloud of dust thrown up, couldn't see properly what had happened at first, but then I saw him. The blast had thrown him to the ground, he was sprawled there, on his back, blood....well, you can imagine. I thought for a second he was dead, killed outright. The lads were roarin': "Sarge, it's the Sarge". Shoutin' on the blower for a medevac, rushing forward, to help him like, but I had to hold them, steady, lads, you don't know if there's others. They do that, the bastards, get one of us then wait for the others to rush into help before detonating another one, getting more of us. But I see he's still alive, in a very bad way, but alive. And he's talking, calling out you'd say but I'd say more like talking, talking to you, Andy, son. He's calling out your name, "Andrew, Andrew". Some of the lads think he's calling for one of them but no one had that name and I knew he was talking about you. So I go over to him and he's in a bad way. I do what I can to patch him up, we give him morphine, for the pain, but he's not looking at me, he's looking over my shoulder or off to the side someways and he's talking to you, just like I'm talking to you right now, I swear to God. And that gave him comfort, son, I swear to God it did. He called out for you and you were there, at least to him, you were. And he called you his beautiful boy, and said that he never wanted to leave you. Those were his last words on this earth, God rest his soul.'

I could feel hot tears flowing down my cheeks, almost burning my skin. There were tears in Sgt. Pearse's eyes too, as he whipped out a hanky from somewhere and honked his nose, noisily, almost funnily. My mother slid in beside me and hugged me and kissed my cheek. I knew she was crying too. We sat there for a few minutes, the early dark of a winter afternoon wrapping around us.

CHAPTER NINE

Last Sunday of Advent

The events of Saturday cast a shadow over the rest of the week-end. Even though I had asked him to tell me about it, the images of my father's death described by Sgt. Pearse were now seared into my brain, in full HD, 3-D vision. I could not close my eyes without seeing him lying there, in the dirt, calling out for me, dying of his wounds. I suppose I had imagined such things before but somehow the fact of them got pushed to the back of my mind. Now they were right there and refused to be displaced by anything else. Mum and I hugged each other after Sgt. Pearse left to return home to his family that evening. I think even for her, the description of the scene of his death was hard to bear. They had, after all, loved each other once. And I knew my Mum was soft-hearted and couldn't bear to think of anything or anyone in pain.

Uncle Edward and Gran joined us for dinner that evening, pre-planned by my Mum, just in case of such an eventuality. And I was glad to see them this time. I needed the comfort of them and even the normality of their presence to try to help me get back to the here and now as my brain refused to budge from Afghanistan and the dirty track of earth where my father had met his end. In some ways, this felt like when we had just learned of his death in the summer. But this was more visceral somehow, maybe because of the eye-witness testimony or maybe because Sgt. Pearse's stories had, in some way, brought my father back to life so it felt like I was losing him all over again.

Gran sat with me in the living room while Mum made dinner in the kitchen, Uncle Edward 'helping' her. Gran chatted as only Gran could but I enjoyed her distracting chatter for once. But she too was extra careful to be kind to me, holding my hand in hers, comparing her knarled old rheumatic hands to mine, complimenting me on my long, slender fingers, like a pianist's or a surgeon's, smiling at me as she said that.

'Your Dad and me didn't get on all that well, especially towards the end, y'know, Andrew. But I don't doubt for one minute he loved you very much. I know he was difficult, and a big feckin' eejit at times too, especially with the drink in him, but I think deep down he was just confused or unhappy or something. War changes people, I know that much. Even back in the old days, with the Troubles, I saw it myself then. Mothers lose sons, boys become men because of bloodshed and it scars them. The pain radiates all round and through people. God alone knows the sort of things your father saw out there. I know he never really talked about it, not to us, anyway. But it must often have been terrible. I've prayed on it, Andrew, I don't mind telling you that, and have confessed it too, God help me, that I didn't show him enough compassion, that I turned my back on him when maybe he just needed a hand of friendship or support, I don't know. But I couldn't get beyond the harm he was causing to your mother, and to you. But I regret it now, Andrew, God knows I do.' Gran reached into her handbag to fetch a tattered tissue to dab her eyes and her nose.

'Don't get upset, Gran. I think he knew how you felt about him and he respected you for standing up for your daughter, and for me, too. He even told me as much, once.'

Gran dabbed her nose, composing herself again. 'He always did spin yarns, that fella!' We both giggled a bit, knowing full well the enmity between Dad and Gran was legendary. If Mum was fiery, she was only a spark from the original as Gran in high dudgeon could stop tanks in their tracks. Her fury was a force of nature and nothing riled her more than someone harming her daughter. I know Dad did bad things, even though everyone did their best to hide them from me. But towards the end of their marriage, there had been violence. I know Mum had been hit, so hard in fact she lost some hearing in her right ear permanently. I think that had been the final straw, especially for Gran who railed that her husband had never lifted a hand to her in all their married life together and that any man who did was no man at all, soldier or not, no matter what he'd been through. I tended to agree with her then but I suppose it's also true that sometimes people who are damaged themselves have a hard time controlling their emotions. Dad certainly did and lashed out over often trivial things. He accused Mum of nagging him when she asked him to do perfectly reasonable things and usually added 'just like your bloody mother', which really upset her. Perhaps he had PTSD, perhaps he should have seen someone like Medusa, perhaps the army should have supported him better, but all that was academic now. I think Gran did genuinely wish she'd ended on better terms with Dad than she had but I don't think she would ever condone harm being done to her daughter, or me, whatever the extenuating circumstances.

Raised voices came from the kitchen, Mum and Uncle Edward having some sort of row, it sounded like. Gran mumbled something about it being an upsetting day for all but I decided to go and investigate as I suspected I was the source of the argument. As I approached the kitchen door, made of frosted glass, I could see Uncle Edward remonstrating with Mum, his voice raised. I could make out now his words more clearly and he was saying something about how Mum should have intervened and stopped Sgt. Pearse telling me 'all the gory details.'

'I asked him to!' I said calmly, opening the door. Uncle Edward looked at me, straight in the eye, his stare taking me in, our eyes the same deep, watery blue. 'I wanted to know what happened. I needed to know it, no matter how hard it is to hear it.'

Uncle Edward softened his tone, using his 'doctor's voice', full of concern but also authority. 'Andrew, you've been through a lot, especially in the last few weeks. Hearing grisly details about the circumstances of your father's death may not have been the best thing for you right now. It could be upsetting for you.'

'My father dying was upsetting for me. How he died doesn't change the fact of his death. I know it was horrible to hear about him, lying there, in pain, bleeding to death in that terrible place. But Sgt. Pearse also told me that he'd called out for me. He was thinking of me, at the end. For a long time now I wasn't even sure if he cared about me, after everything that happened between him and Mum. But he did care, he really cared, when it mattered. And I'm glad I know about that, even if the rest of it was just horrible to listen to...' At that point my voice cracked and the tears welled up in my eyes, bloody waterworks, always letting me down, unmanning me. Uncle Edward stepped forward and before I realised what was happening he hugged me, held me to him and just hugged me hard. I was a bit thrown at first but somehow it felt really good and just what I needed. I relaxed into it and let him hold me for a few minutes. I felt Mum join us then, and we all stood there, sniffling and crying quietly together as a family, and it felt good, like something had been changed between us all for the better.

Sunday brought frost, ice and Ash, standing cocooned in coat, hat, scarf, gloves and boots, shivering on the door-step. Ash did not like the cold. He almost jumped inside when I opened the door to him, saying it was bloody freezing and pulling off his big boots before I could even get a hello out. He unwrapped the various layers surrounding him so when finally revealed he appeared to be half the size he had been when he'd entered. Mum was out with Gran, having driven her to church for Sunday Mass, the last before Christmas. She was then going into town to finish up some Christmas shopping, she'd said. So we had the house to ourselves, unusual enough so we took advantage of having unimpeded access to the living room and TV. Ash had brought round a couple of DVDs for us to watch, both things I had seen before but good enough not to mind watching again. When we had settled down on the sofa watching the latest in the *Star Trek* franchise, a re-imagined prequel to the original series, drinking cokes and munching crisps, Ash got to the real point of visit and asked me how I'd gotten on the day before with my 'visitor'. I felt strangely put out by his question, like he was intruding into something private although I realised he was only asking out of genuine concern. But I decided not to tell him about finding out about how my Dad had died. Instead, I decided to show him the things Sgt. Pearse had brought home. I insisted he washed his hands first though as they were covered in disgusting grease from the crisps we'd been scoffing. He harrumphed but did it anyway. He was really impressed by the campaign medals. I tried to recount their meaning as best as I could remember from what Sgt. Pearse had told me about them.

'I never realised your Dad had been so many places and done so many brave things.' I basked in his praise, pleased that he was impressed which was not something you saw every day with Ash.

'There was something else, a photograph.' I handed Ash the photo of Dad and me, the one taken in Forbury Park.

'The Maiwand Lion!' Ash echoed my own surprise.

'I didn't even remember it until I saw it yesterday. It was taken on my birthday when we first moved to Reading. Apparently, Dad used to touch it for luck before every mission and after he came back.' Ash continued to stare at the picture, recognising the importance the object now had for me. This had been my Dad's talisman, his good luck charm to keep him safe from harm.

'But it's the Lion, Andrew. Don't you see it?'

'Yes, I know. That's what I'm saying. I completely forgot that he had that with him. If you'd asked me I would even have said I'd never really noticed the Lion before, well, what happened in November but it's always been there, in the background, sort of. My Dad looked at that picture every day when he was out in the field.'

'That's it, exactly,' Ash looked at me excitedly. 'That's why the Lion has such significance for you, because of this. Even though you'd forgotten about it, your Dad probably mentioned it to you, maybe years ago, and that's why, when you saw it on Remembrance Sunday, it sparked a memory deep within your unconscious mind and that led to....'

'My little episode?' I jumped in to relieve Ash of the struggle to find a suitable euphemism. 'Maybe, that could be it. But I tell you, I really had forgotten all about it, the whole day, not just the picture of the Lion. I guess because things went so downhill between Mum and Dad after that time I must have edited it out of my mind. Although I can't think why. It was one of the nicest days we'd had together as a family in recent times. It was my twelfth birthday. I started secondary school that September. That's when I first met you.' We both grinned at the shared memory of our first meeting at school, 'nerds of a feather, flocking together'.

The movie played out, the theme being time travel to try to avenge a wrong done by travelling back to intervene before the event. If only things like that were possible, I thought. Maybe on that lovely summer's day those few years ago, I could appear to myself, in front of the Lion and warn everyone of what was going to happen, convince my Dad to retire from the Army, not to go to Afghanistan in 2009. But would it have made any difference even if I could have done such an impossible thing. As Sgt. Pearse had said, once it's your turn there's no avoiding it. And maybe the universe is set up like that, to take account of all possible eventualities and yet still deliver the same outcome. So it wasn't like the multi-verse Ash has described where all possibilities were played out but rather a literal universe where the story unravelled exactly as it should do, no matter how we tried to intervene. Those thoughts swirled around my brain as I watched the very young Captain James T. Kirk struggle to overcome his enemies' timeline altering attack, aided and abetted by his old/new friend Spock, both the very young and very old versions in the same movie. Things like this made my head ache a little. But reality was much simpler. If you're dead, you're dead. There is no time travel, and things like that cannot be undone, however much you might wish for a second chance.

It was dark before four PM that afternoon, a leaden sky adding to the pre-Christmas gloom. Mum arrived back just as the credits for the movie were rolling, shouting for help to unload the car. She'd been shopping, and was carefully carrying something in one of those suit-carriers they give you in *John Lewis* when you buy something substantial and posh. As it was nearly Christmas, I didn't ask what she'd bought as I thought that maybe it was a surprise so I just got on with fetching the rest of the bags from the boot, Ash assisting but over-acting the effects the short-exposure to the cold had on his delicate constitution.

Mum had bought food as well and asked Ash if he'd like to stay for a proper Sunday 'lunch', roast potatoes and all. We normally had only two meals on Sundays as Mum only did 'brunch' which usually consisted of boiled eggs and toast so by the time it was late afternoon I was certainly happy to hear we had the prospect of a proper dinner. Mum could be a good cook when she put her mind to it but during the week we lived off microwave meals as she was too tired from work to cook anything and I couldn't be arsed doing anything more than beans on toast. Ash looked at me for permission to accept the invitation, sensitive as always not to overstay his welcome. But I was glad that he'd been asked as I didn't want another 'intense' family meal with my Mum. I sensed she also wanted to avoid anything too onerous as she seemed much more upbeat than she'd been in recent days. Spending money always had that effect on her. She wasn't exactly prodigal but she did enjoy a good old splurge when given the chance, especially if she was buying fancy clothes or shoes or perfume. From the number of *John Lewis* bags I brought in from the car, I suspected she'd battered the credit card to within an inch of its life.

We spent the remainder of the evening pleasantly enough, a mixture of helping Mum prepare the meal, eating too much and playing computer games. I checked my e-mails and Facebook page to see if there was any news of Natasha but there wasn't so I figured I'd check in with her the next day at school anyway. It was about 9.30 PM when Ash's Dad came by to pick him up. He cracked some terrible jokes as usual during his short visit to our house. Mum invited him in for coffee but he politely declined saying as it was a school night he'd better get 'this young man to bed', causing Ash to blush behind his specs and everyone to smile as his discomfiture. So the whole week-end ended on a nice normal note, as if the events of the previous day hadn't really happened. And that was what I really wanted more than anything, just to be normal, eat Sunday dinner, mess around with Ash, watch movies and play computer games. But as I lay there in my bed, trying to find sleep, from deep within my mind, images came, unbidden, drifting up to the front of my brain, of blood and pain and the Maiwand Lion.

CHAPTER TEN

Winter Solstice

We had our English term test that Monday morning, the last of the Christmas exams. I had been very relaxed about it as English was my best subject and these exams weren't really important anyway, just 'indicative' as Brennan reminded us while urging us to treat them seriously. The questions were pretty much as predicted and ones I had done practice answers on before. There was the usual one about the significance of the appearance of the ghost of Hamlet's father although my recent experiences had sensitised me a little to the theme and this was reflected in my answer, improving it from previous attempts I felt. But even during the exam, thoughts of the Maiwand Lion and its significance to me were not far from my mind, especially after the revelations of the week-end. At lunchtime there was the usual chatter in the school canteen about the paper and answers to the questions. I noticed Natasha huddled at a corner table with three of her mates. She seemed upset. I couldn't believe that she'd done as bad as all that. She did well in English usually, Brennan even reading out some of her essays to the whole class on occasion, mortifying Nat of course who didn't like drawing that sort of attention to herself, although she was far from a shrinking violet normally. I asked Ash if he knew why she was so upset but he shrugged and muttered something about it being best not to get involved. But I didn't like to think of Natasha being upset, especially as she'd been so kind to me since my Dad's death. I decided to risk it and approach the table she was at, her friends ringed around it like Macbeth's witches around a cauldron. One of them noticed me approaching and stiffened, alerting the others. Natasha looked up at me, smiling weakly but her eyes red from crying. Tracey Mellors brusquely asked me what I wanted but I ignored her and asked Nat directly if she was ok. She said she would be. I told her not to worry about the stupid test, that it didn't really count for anything anyway and given her course work she had nothing to worry about even if it went badly. She sort of laughed a little sarcastically, saying that test was the least of her worries. Tracey Mellors then told me to sod off and leave them alone. The others closed ranks around Nat who smiled at me telling me she was fine, not to worry and that she'd catch up with me later, effectively dismissing me. I was a bit taken aback by this but decided not to force the issue and said something about hoping she'd be OK whatever was wrong and that I'd catch up with her later.

Ash had completely missed my absence from the table we'd been sharing, engrossed in his PSP as usual and didn't even notice my return for a bit until I reached over and covered the screen he was looking at with my hand.

'There's definitely something wrong with Natasha,' I whispered to him. He looked slightly glazed behind his specs and said without a flicker of change in his expression, 'It's probably because she's pregnant.' I looked at him to see if he was joking, which would have been both uncharacteristic and rather crude of him and when I saw he was simply relating a fact to me in his typical Vulcan way, I asked him what the hell he was talking about.

'I heard Tracey Mellors telling Casey Grant about it when we were queuing for lunch.' I had to let the news sink in for a few seconds before deciding if what Ash was telling me was probable. I glanced over towards Natasha's table again and saw both Casey Grant and Tracey Mellors still huddled together, forming a protective shield around Nat. So it must be true, at least that made sense of what I was seeing and how Nat was behaving. Ash continued: 'I heard them talking about it in the lunch queue. Girls like Tracey and Casey don't even notice blokes like me. We're sort of invisible to them, as if we inhabit another plane of existence. So they talk to each other about private things without even considering the possibility of being overheard. After all, you don't worry about an eavesdropper you don't even think exists.'

Even allowing for Ash's rather fanciful description, it did sound entirely plausible that those two air-heads would talk about something like that in front of him without thinking twice. And it would explain both Natasha's recent 'illness' and her being upset. Ash went on to say that it happened at Tracey's 16th birthday party when Nat got off with Jimmy Jackson.

'I thought he was going out with Casey?'

'Nah, they broke up shortly after Natasha's 16th birthday. Don't you read people's relationship status on Facebook?'

'I've been a bit distracted lately with my own stuff!'

'Anyway, that's what's going on. All a bit *Hollyoaks*, if you ask me. But I feel sorry for Natasha. Imagine what a kid of Jimmy Jackson's will look like- they better check all his fingers and toes twice for webbing!'

I couldn't help but laugh a bit at Ash's comments, delivered dryly as ever so you had to think twice about whether it was meant as a joke or not. A part of me felt a little betrayed by Nat if I'm honest. While I never really entertained any serious prospect of us getting together, I still thought maybe she did. The fact that she'd moved on completely and in such a serious way made me consider again how out of touch I was with everyone. I also felt so immature and childish. I had not been with anyone in that way, not even come close. Everyone else seemed to be growing up and getting on with their lives all around me while I was stuck in some perpetual Peter Pan existence, worrying about moving statues and their meanings. For Ash, I knew, the whole situation with Nat would be of anthropological interest only and he didn't really care or show any interest in things like sex in more than the most cursory way. Perhaps he was more resigned to his nerd status than me or perhaps his parents' strict moral code meant that such considerations were off the table for him until he was much older. I sort of wished for his certainty and lack of concern about such matters. I felt like I was between worlds, the 'normals' and the 'nerds', which was probably the worst place to be. I glanced over at Natasha again. She was leaving the table with her 'bodyguard' now but saw me look at her and gave me a weak smile. A roar of laughter from the other side of the canteen caught both our attentions. Jimmy Jackson was the source, surrounded by his mates, cracked up by something hilarious. Nat looked down and her friends formed an escort around her ushering her away.

Leaving school at four o'clock that day, the darkness was already falling and so was the snow. At first, the large lazy fluffy flakes falling down seemed unthreatening and a seasonal note on which to begin the holidays as school broke up for the Christmas so we were in good form as we trudged down the road to town. But our enjoyment soon turned to mild anxiety as we realised that the unrelenting cascade of snow was quickly building up, laying down a deep, perfect layer of whiteness on everything with amazing speed. From the time we left school to reaching town, there were at least six inches of snow on the pavement and the roads, muffling the usual traffic noise and bringing everything slowly but noticeably to a full stop. On reaching our usual bus stop by St. Mary Butts Church, we noticed that the air tasted bitter with the fumes of hundreds of cars, lorries and buses idling their engines as the usually snarled traffic came to a complete halt. No one and nothing was moving except the snow which fell and fell and fell without let up and with a laid-back determination to transform Reading into something more typical of Siberia. We decided that we would be better off risking walking than being buried in a snow drift waiting for a bus that would never turn up and even if it did would be going nowhere unless it transformed into a helicopter. By the time we reached the railway station, the snow was so deep we had to walk like we were wading through mud, picking up our feet before gingerly taking the next step and plunging down into the deep drifts covering everywhere. There was no wind but the snowfall was so heavy the whole town appeared as if it was encased in one of those snow globes you seen in tacky gift stores at Christmas. Through the virtual white-out of a million million snowflakes, I saw him peering through it all towards me, the Maiwand Lion, his massive grey iron mane now crowned with inches of snow, adding to his bulk and majesty. But even his great mass did not stay in sight long as we shuffled gratefully toward the shelter of the railway bridge, giving us a respite from the snow trek, and allowing us to shake clumps of snow from our shoes. My feet were now frozen as I had only worn my usual school shoes, black brogues, whose only saving grace were their rubber soles which at least allowed me to stay standing upright. Ash had been more circumspect and clumped along in his big boots. I congratulated him on his foresight but he admitted this had been good luck rather than good planning as the snow fall we were fighting through had not been predicted by the local BBC weather forecast that morning. We sneered about how useless the forecasters were which gave Ash an opening to opine on one of his favourite topics, chaos theory and how the beating of the wings of a butterfly in Brazil could cause a snow storm in Berkshire. I rolled my eyes in a heard it all before sort of way but at the back of my mind I did mull over how the most insignificant things we did or thought could have impacts so important it was hard to believe their source was so banal. When you look at the sequence of events in your life sometimes you see how very fundamental parts of your existence owe their being to random small acts and decisions. Like my being here at all was due to a decision my Mum made about some bloke she saw at a club she went to when she was a student, fancied, shagged and then there was me. And how the decision of a 16 year old boy to join up eventually cost him his life in a parched piece of earth in Afghanistan. I wonder if either of them knew the consequences of their little decisions would they have made the same choices. You could go mad thinking about things like that.

As we trudged forward again across the roundabout and over Reading Bridge, cars snaked along beside us at a snail's pace, idling their engines frustrated, their drivers torn between the relative warmth and comfort of their metal cocoon, and the temptation to abandon their vehicles and takes their chances by walking like us. Fumes from a thousand exhausts added a bitter under-taste to the flavour of snow melting on my tongue as I looked up and opened my mouth to receive the large white flakes like the Host. My face was kissed by a hundred flakes in seconds and my eyelids were closed by snow like pennies on a corpse. All that was familiar became strange. The usual topography of my route home, which I must have walked a hundred thousand times was rendered alien by the heavy obfuscation of snow. The normal traffic noises were transformed into a low, throbbing undertone to accompany the amazing visuals of the snowfall. It was like a scene from one of those American disaster movies but on a more pedestrian and English scale, the ordinary rendered extraordinary by the commonplace event of snow in December.

Ash and I had ceased commenting on the difficult progress of our journey by the time we had trudged past Caversham laundry as we ran out of appropriate expressions of amazement at the scene we were witnessing and saved our breath for the increasing ordeal of putting one foot in front of the other. By the time we reached the bottom of Donkin Hill, we were so knackered it appeared to us as if we were approaching Everest from the base-camp. We both looked at each other and smiled weakly for mutual encouragement as we set out to conquer our mountain, because it was there and because we had no choice to go around. On reaching the summit, and attaining the level plateau of Henley Road, we both laughed, stimulated by our great achievement and the giddy excitement that all humans feel having overcome the insurmountable. We parted company outside the Co-op, and I set off on my lone trek home the remaining few hundred meters with the grim determination of Scott of the Antarctic.

I can't tell you the sense of joy I had on opening my front door and stepping inside, pulling off my cold, clammy shoes and socks and absorbing the warmth of the carpet through my bare feet. I peeled off my sodden overcoat, now virtually white all over the back except for the patch my rucksack had covered. The vibration of my phone in my pocket let me know that Ash had made it through the snow too in one piece and was likewise relieved to be home and dry. I climbed up the stairs to my room and stripped down to my underwear, chucking my damp school uniform into the laundry basket with some satisfaction that I wouldn't need to worry about having it clean again until next year. And so it was that I found myself almost naked staring out my bedroom window at the strange sight of trees bent under the weight of their white burden, the boundary between hedges, lawns and foot-paths obscured, and houses along the road cowering under caps of snow. The amber light from the street lamps and the hushed funeral cortege of traffic added to the strangeness of the sight. It was as alien a view as if I had been somehow transported to another country or perhaps more appropriate to say that an alien climate had imposed its hold over my country, like the red weed from Mars covering England like a blood-stain in H.G. Wells' *'War of the Worlds'*.

The hypnotic hold the scene had over me was only broken when I saw the familiar figure of my mother making her way up the snow-bound drive-way, sheltering under her red umbrella and leaning on someone's arm, some man's arm, his face hidden under her brolly too. But somehow I know all too well who was on her arm. I was at the top of the stairs in my dressing gown when the front door opened, my mother and the plonker falling through it in a tumble of laughter and breathlessness. His shoulders wore snow epaulettes, her face flushed with the effort of their journey home. She clocked me a second or so later, as she was brushing the snow of his shoulders. Her voice was laced with laughter as she looked up to where I stood.

'Hello, luv! You made it home, too.'

'And without a team of huskies, either!' Jonathan chimed in, laughing at his own joke. I didn't respond but Mum continued in a lilting jolly tone as she recounted how they'd been forced to abandon attempts to drive home by the snow even before trying to set out from their offices in town as they 'would have needed snow shovels just to get the car park!'

'And poor Jonathan is stranded!' she continued. 'The traffic is simply snowed in so there's no way he's going to be able to make it back to Pangbourne, not tonight anyway. So I've said he can stay with us tonight, OK?' The words hit me like a slap in the face.

'Whatever!' I turned on my heel and headed back to my bedroom. Mum yelled after me that she'd have dinner ready in an hour or so, maintaining the Doris Day tone in her voice. I could hear the two of them laugh together at some private joke as I shut my bedroom door behind me. Christ, what a fucking cheek, bringing him here, like that. It was obvious he was going to sleep here tonight, and where. I knew they'd been sneaking around together for the past few months but somehow this seemed so blatant, so in your face, so final. My mother had completely 'moved on' from Dad. She had her sights on someone else, now. It was as if my Dad never really existed, like he hadn't mattered. But he had existed, I was living proof of that inconvenient fact for her. He had loved her until the day he died and now, barely cold in his grave, here she was cavorting around in the house his money helped buy. The anger rising up in my chest felt like a heart-attack or something. I couldn't breathe properly, my head pounded with every pulse, my shoulders tightened so hard I had to rub them to ease the pain. I fixed my glare outside, on the snow, the snow falling and falling, obliterating all ugliness with its purity. It's a pity our lives couldn't be purified so easily, erasing all the past with a blanket of white, like a new canvas ready to be painted on, or a page ready for the writer.

Peals of laughter rose up from downstairs, as the two love-birds cooed to each other. Then I heard someone coming upstairs, him, not her, I could tell it wasn't her step, his, heavier, his big frame moving forward. For a moment I thought he was going to come into my room. I froze, ready for the conflict. I could barely hear the sounds he made for the pounding of the blood in my ears. But as the seconds ticked by, I realised, he hadn't come to my door. Perhaps he'd gone to the bathroom. I decided I needed to explore, some compulsion in me forcing me forward. I opened the door to my room and peeked out. There was no one on the short landing. The bathroom door was slightly ajar. Perhaps he'd gone in and hadn't locked it properly. I decided to approach the door, to listen in, I don't know why, something animal in me resented him pissing in my house. But on moving forward a step or two, something at the edge of my peripheral vision caused me to turn around, and there he was, standing by my mother's bed, stark bollock naked, having just stepped out of his pants. He turned around, now facing me, his cock and balls poking from the bird's nest bush of his pubes, his round belly latticed with body hair. He was suddenly aware of me, standing there. He started, looked me straight in the face, with an awkward smile, he said, 'Oops'. Oops, that's what he said, as if he'd spilled some milk he was adding to his tea or something. He made a vague attempt to cover his cock and balls with his hands, but only half-baked. 'I was just changing out of my wet clothes. Got soaked through, coming home in the snow. Your Mum said there was a dressing gown up here I could borrow. Ah, there it is.' He stepped towards the open door. I reacted by stepping back, thought maybe he was moving towards me. 'Pardon me,' he said, as he stood before me naked, opening the robe, my father's robe, the one Mum has bought for him from *John Lewis* a few years before for Christmas. 'All boys together, anyway! Not as if I've got anything you don't, eh?' His stupid public school accent, his complete nonchalance about being found naked, in my mother's bedroom, by me, stunned me for a few seconds. But the sight of him wrapped now in the dressing gown I remembered my father wearing the last Christmas we had spent together properly as a family, completely set me off.

'Get out of that, you fuckin' bastard. That's my Dad's, you prick!' Completely without thinking about it, I flung myself towards him, grabbed the collar of the robe with both hands, and started trying to pull it from him.

'Andrew, for God's sake, calm down, will you!' he shouted. 'Get off me, let go, don't be so stupid!'

But I wouldn't , I pulled the robe over his head, so he was bent over, trying to hang onto the robe and his dignity, both, and unsuccessfully in both cases. 'Fucking bastard, fucking bastard!' I yelled, with increasing anger, wrestling him. He was bigger than me, and stronger, and once he got over the surprise attack, started to fight back, gripping my wrists to disengage my hands from the robe. I was suddenly aware of someone tugging at my elbow, Mum, trying to pull me off him, her voice a mix of anger and shock and fear. Somehow, between them, they broke my grip and I was sent tumbling back, landing on my arse on the floor, staring up at him, covering up his cock and balls with my father's robe. My mother's face was white with fear, the plonker's purple with anger and effort. 'What the hell's gotten into you, Andrew!' my mother yelled, helping the plonker get sorted.

'What's wrong with me? What's wrong with you, y' mean? Bringing that bastard here, standing there, stark bullock naked, wearing Dad's things!'

'For God's sake, Andrew. Grow up, will you. Jonathan got soaked through walking me home through the snow storm. I told him to get out of his wet clothes to get dry and warm so he doesn't catch his death. Your father hardly ever wore this robe and it's the only thing in the house that's suitable.'

'Look, if it's a problem, I can change back,' the plonker, suddenly conciliatory, said to my Mum.

'Maybe you should both just jump into bed together, that'd soon warm you both up!' I jumped up to my feet again, anger flowing through me , directing me, consuming me. 'Why don't you just fuck her, then, Jonathan, eh?' I rushed towards him again, grabbing him by the lapels of the robe, with all my strength. We were engaged in a frantic tug of war for a few seconds, everyone screaming, my Mum pulling at my arm. I broke loose but somehow my elbow caught my Mum's face- she screamed, her hand covered her face, blood trickled down her chin from her cut lip. I froze. I felt terrible, I hadn't meant to hurt her, only him. The tears started then. The plonker put one arm around her shoulder, comforting her, the other he used to pull her hand gently away from her face, to inspect the damage. There was a red mark where my elbow had made impact, her bottom lip was split, blood, scarlet red against her pale, pale skin, flowed down her chin, dripping from her jaw down onto her white blouse, spreading like an inkblot there. The plonker's voice was suddenly soothing, assuring her she'd be okay, advising everyone to just calm down, easing her towards the bed, sitting her down on it, sitting there himself. The robe slipped from him, revealing his cock and balls again.

'Get off her, she's my mother.' I tried to pull him away from her. 'Get away from me, Andrew,' she shouted, tears and anger changing the tone of her voice dramatically. It was cold towards me, hard. 'You've done enough damage for one day. What the hell's gotten into you! You should be ashamed of yourself!'

'Now why don't we all calm down,' plonker intoned, using his lawyerly authority to try to pull things back. 'This is all just a misunderstanding and an accident. Let's get you cleaned up and see what the damage is. You may need stitches. Andrew, where's your first aid kit, please?'

I didn't answer. I felt myself withdrawing, as if watching the scene before me in a movie or something. He moved her towards the bathroom, reassuring her. I could hear her voice, full of tears, pain and anger. There was the sound of running water and his voice telling her everything would be OK, kind, calming. I suddenly knew I couldn't be there anymore, I needed to go, get out, and leave the place contaminated by the presence of my mother and her lover, desecrating the house she had shared with my father. I went to my room, pulled on a t-shirt, jeans and a thick Aran sweater my Gran had bought me for Christmas the year before then I went back to the landing, planning to dart downstairs and out the door while they were in the bathroom, but she was standing there, pale, her lip purple, her hand white holding white toilet paper to the cut in her lip, her eyes wide, glaring at me, angry.

'Proud of yourself, Andrew? You really are your father's son!' Poison dripped from her tongue, acid in the words she sprayed at me, intending to sting. For a second, I was paralysed with the impact her words and her face made on me. But then the anger glowed red again.

'Don't mention his name! You're not fit to mention his name!' I shouted at her, hot tears welling up in my eyes, my voice strained because I was talking about him. 'You're probably glad he's dead so you can get on...' Before I finished my words, a sharp, hot, searing blow silenced my mouth. She had slapped me across the face with such force I was shocked into silence for a second. Her voice was tight like a bow-string, hissing at me: 'Don't you ever speak to me like that about your father ever again, do you hear? Never!'

I couldn't believe what was happening, how things were spiralling out of control. Mum and I glared at each other like two sworn enemies, rage pumping through us like steroids. In that moment she ceased to be my Mum and just became this woman I barely knew. I saw her eyes, cold blue, burn with anger, her lips, bleeding red, form words of spite and her hands, clenched white-knuckled, shake with fury. I thought, this is the last time I'll see your face, the last time you'll see mine. I suddenly realised I had come to the end of my time in this house, no longer my home, and the end of the time I would spend seeing this woman as any sort of mother. I ran down the stairs, quickly pulled on my boots, my coat, my scarf and left, slamming the front door behind me. I listened out for it but failed to hear any voice shout after me not to go. So pulling my coat around me, pulling on my gloves, and tightening my boot-laces, I set off into the snow, the incessantly falling snow, into the night, with no plan and no place to go to but one, where he was, where he stood, the Maiwand Lion.

CHAPTER ELEVEN

Pilgrimage

The anger kept me warm, at first. I trudged through the snow-bound streetscape, strangely quiet, alien, the houses huddled together for warmth. I was burning with fury, angry at everything and everyone, my stupid mother for her stupid boyfriend, even my father for being stupid enough to get himself killed and allow all this crap to happen to us. My thoughts were all over the place, I didn't have any plan but to go to where he was, the Lion. I briefly considered calling on Ash but dismissed it. What was the point? He wouldn't understand how I was feeling. In his ordered world of logic, emotions like mine right then were as unlikely as an elephant at the Arctic, the two things simply had no business being together. So I trudged on, glad of the space, the silence, the lack of people and traffic, just me and the snow. It sort of felt like a disaster movie again, with me, the sole survivor, heading out in the unknown, the transformed world where all certainties had vanished. My breath formed a fog in front of my face, my hands were shoved deep into my pockets as I strode forward. But I was forced to take them out again to help me balance when the snow became slippery underfoot as I descended Donkin Hill, walking on the road instead of the footpath to avoid the deepest snow but this traffic-compacted stuff brought its own challenges and I slid like Bambi on the ice.

It the going got easier in when I got onto the level of Bryant Avenue. As I shuffled onwards, I began to glimpse into some houses where the people inside hadn't yet drawn their curtains. Christmas trees blinked and winked at me from some windows, TV screens illuminated others with their electric blue light. I saw the faces of families, huddled together on sofas around their favourite programmes, comfortingly warm against the cold outside, like cave-men around a camp-fire. But I was on the outside looking in. This was how I often felt. I never really fitted in, not completely. I frequently felt like an observer in my own life, not fully invested, watching things unfold like a TV show I was only half interested in. Even as I walked along the white quiet streets of Caversham that night, I sort of saw myself as if I was watching myself from outside my body. I don't mean like I was spaced out or something but I kind of felt not quite inside my own head. I could see myself, this boy, walking through the snow, down the deserted streets, under the orange glow of the street lights. I could feel the cold on my face, in my feet, seeping through my coat so clearly I was still in my body. But some part of me remained apart, saw me like it was watching me from across the street. Maybe that was my soul, maybe it's just how we remember things, like when you're in a dream and you can see yourself from above or something.

It was slow going because of the snow and the cold started to really sting my nose and my ears and my toes. But I couldn't contemplate just turning back and going home, with him there, no doubt his arms around her, comforting her, telling her what a terrible son I was and that she had no reason to blame herself. Her, with her vicious words and evil stare, glaring at me. My face still stung where her hand had hit me. I fancied there was even a red welt in the shape of a hand there, a scarlet mark of shame. I couldn't believe how things had gone and yet, somehow, they seemed utterly predictable. She had not really been there for me since Dad died or not at least in the way I wanted or needed. I felt like she had removed herself from the situation, like I was the only one really grieving, and even I felt fake about it sometimes, given how things had gone between Dad and me the last time we'd seen each other. But for her, her dead husband was just another fact of her existence, something to be 'gotten over' so she could 'move on with her life'. For me, I could never have another father, so I couldn't replace the one I'd lost with someone else, no matter how much my mother might think I could. And I certainly wouldn't accept her choice for the job. I couldn't stand the plonker and I knew he didn't like me either, no matter how much he tried to pretend he did for my mother's sake. The thoughts of the two of them together made my blood boil. I couldn't bear to think of it but now it had been rubbed in my face.

I reached the place where you could divert down to the river instead of following along the road, just opposite the church on Gosbrook Road. I decided on impulse to head down the side-road towards the Thames path. The snow there was even deeper as it had not been trodden down or driven on to any extent. It came over the top of my boots, wetting the bottom of my trousers. I was aware of that but somehow was becoming a bit immune to it. The cold was just another fact now, like breathing, or hearing the pulsing of blood in my ears. Before long, I was walking alongside the black flowing river. The noise of the cascade by the weir was Niagara-like in the cold silence. I looked up towards Reading Bridge, its elegant stone arc leaping from bank to bank, sturdy like that for maybe a hundred years now. This scene, the river, the bridge, the moon, could have been seen pretty much exactly like this by a boy like me during World War One. I stood for a few minutes to catch my breath, to gather my thoughts. My feet took me to the edge of the river bank, under a willow tree leaning into the river as if to admire its own reflection. I listened to the water move, coursing onwards towards London. It didn't care what was going on around it. It just flowed like it always had. Maybe Roman soldiers had stood on this spot, centuries ago, and watched this same river on a winter's night just before Saturnalia when Hadrian was Emperor. I watched the river move, undulate, light reflecting from its surface, from the brilliant white moon peeping through gaps in the black clouds and from the few buildings lit up on the opposite bank. It was hypnotic, the sound, the shapes, the slip-slide of time and tide. I could just ease myself into it. I imagined the shock of the cold water, the rush of breath from my lungs. I imagined the change in sounds as my head submerged below the surface. I imagined the green grey light as I opened my eyes. I imagined bubbles floating in front of my face as the last breath left my body. I imagined the metallic taste of the water as I inhaled the cold river into my lungs. I wondered would I panic and fight for life or just resign myself to death and fall into the blackness. I wondered if I would know if I was dead. Or would it be just nothingness? But what if there was something, something better than this, or something worse? This thought caused me to pause and pulled me back from the brink. I thought of my Dad. His life was over now, taken from him. He'd had no choice in that, not really. Could I just throw mine away? Or maybe I'd see him there, waiting for me. Would he be happy to see me, knowing I was dead, too? Or would he be angry with me that I'd cut my own life short? I shivered with cold. I heard a fox cry. I felt snowflakes land on my cheeks, and tears, warm, slide down my face. An icy breeze from the river ruffled my hair and suddenly I knew I needed to push on, to see the Lion and bring my thoughts and pain to him, like an offering. I don't know if I expected anything more than his silence but I knew I needed to see him.

So I started out again, climbing the slope from the river to the bridge, breathless on getting to the top, back to road level, the effort made difficult by the deep snow. And then my phone rang, Ash's name flashing at me from the screen as I looked at it in my hand, not sure whether to answer or not. It stopped ringing. I switched it off. I didn't want anyone or anything to spoil this moment for me, to take the magic out of it with logic. I walked on, over the bridge, my steps more determined than ever, as I felt him draw me close. I started to run or at least stumbled forward more quickly over the snow, falling over a few times but just picking myself up and pushing on. It wasn't long before I'd reached the red-brick wall surrounding his domain, Forbury Park, dark and silent, and him, stark against the sky, a line of deep snow along his back and mane etching his form out from the blackness, so he looked dramatically real, like I was seeing him through 3-D glasses.

The gates of the park were locked, but it only took a little effort to clamber over the Victorian brickwork wall, out of sight of prying eyes, round by the side opposite the old grave-yard, completely silent and alone, just me and him. I landed onto pure virgin snow on the other side of the wall, the landing jolting the breath out of my body. I stood up and just took him in, the size of him, the shape of him, slowly approaching him, as if he were real, like he might suddenly startle and leap forward on hearing my approach. But he didn't, he remained perfectly solid and still. I kept my eyes fixed on him all the same, circling around so that I was facing him directly, his head raised in that silent roar he'd cried for more than a century, frozen in time.

I remember just standing there, looking at him. I can't remember for how long exactly, I just know that I stood there, looking at him, transfixed, thinking about that day in November when I first saw him move, heard him roar, felt the impact of his power in my chest so hard that it knocked me of my feet. And I remember thinking, well, here I am, what now? Part of me felt stupid, standing there in a field of snow, all alone, apart from him, the two of us just staring at each other. I remember asking myself, what does he want with me, what do you want with me? I mean, this can't all be for nothing. I know I saw you move. I know I saw you roar. I don't care what anyone else thinks about this, I know this was real. I didn't imagine what happened. Doesn't matter what a whole team of shrinks say. It had happened, but only I saw it. But that didn't mean it didn't happen. It was just meant for me. So what do you want with me? What are you trying to tell me? What do you want me to do? Do you want to hurt me, or help me? What is it? Go on, tell me, tell me. Don't just fuck with my head like that, tell me what you want. Is this about my Dad? Is it? What about him? What do you know? Is he all right now, is he with me, watching me, or just no where? Are you with him, somehow? Can you talk to him? Can I talk to him? Why don't you answer? Don't pretend you can't hear me, or understand me? I know you can. So stop being such a bastard and talk to me again. I know you can. I know you did. What are you trying to tell me? Why don't you answer? Why does no one answer? Where's my Dad? Where is he? Where is my Dad? You know, tell me, for God's sake, just tell me he's OK, he's not in pain, tell me? I know you know, somehow, you know. So tell me! Tell me!

The snow had started to really fall again, thousands and thousands of white flakes flying around, driven now by an icy wind, creating a halo around the Lion's mane, his face and head. The snow stung my eyes, made them water, the wind buffeted me, made me cold, made me shiver. So at first I thought that's what I was seeing, because the snow in my eyes and the wind causing tears to well up made it hard to see his face clearly, that's why his mane appeared to move a little, it was just because of that. But as the strength of the wind grew, and the snow swirled around us, between us, I realised his head, which had been looking steadfastly forward had somehow changed its angle, and that his eyes were now looking down, straight into mine. And his mane flowed, just like before, his mouth opened wider, his muscled shoulders moved and strained and I knew, I knew this was really happening, it was really happening. I felt my knees buckle with fear. He looked straight at me, his eyes burned even in the darkness, even through the blizzard whirling around us, and he roared, like the sound of an avalanche, his great roar enveloped me, resounded in my head and my chest, caused my heart to pound erratically, my brain to fire a thousand thousand neurons all at once, and fear like the terror of death to grip my throat so the scream I tried to scream died there. And the noise, the noise hurt my ears, my head and made my body shake. I got that strange taste in my mouth again, like I did on Remembrance Sunday, the metallic acrid taste so strange and yet familiar. And the smell, like something burning but not something normal, something strange, and the feeling of grit in my mouth, like sand between my teeth, and the noise, like a thunder clap going off right beside me or within me, too much, I felt myself thrown back, my body arc through the air and I waited for death.

CHAPTER TWELVE

Dreams of Sangin

The next sensation was of tremendous pressure, forcing all the air out of my lungs. A dull thud was the only noise. I heard all sounds as if underwater. Then the sound of rain. But not rain, earth, falling down all around, pitter-patter on the ground. Occasional differences in pitch as the size of the clods of clay changed. Then an awareness of colour: its absence initially, feeling as if I was in milky tea. Then the ridiculous red revealed as the dust settled on the raised arm before me, my arm, the burning crimson colour of my coat. Would never have called it crimson before, the dull familiar garment but the contrast with the dun dust was so vivid only words like scarlet, vermillion, and claret would do, or ruddy, bloody, red like blood. Then the heat, then the taste and the dryness, dust in the mouth, up the nose, in the eyes. Tears welled up, to wash the face and clear the eyes. Blinking rapidly, to rid the dirt and debris from my brimming eyes, I heard myself coughing, spitting, hawking up clods and clots of earth and sand from my parched throat. Then the sky, cobalt blue, emerging suddenly from the haze as the dust cloud dissipated, a cruel imitation of fog on a summer's day. Then the noises, far away, like an animal, roaring, screaming, yelling, calling, speaking. Words emerging, several voices now, fuck, fuck, fuck, fuck, fuck, oh my fucking fuck, Sarge, Sarge. Still distant but getting nearer. And then the focus of eyes on shapes, getting orientated, getting to understand up from down. Then seeing it, me, lying down, on a road of dust and stones, prone, looking at my own arm, dust and blood red. And something else, a shape carved from the earth, the same hue but emerging as distinct, shapes coming into focus not made by nature, lines, curves, forms of belts and buckles and pockets and straps and then the crimson and black of blood on khaki.

Then the movements, frantic, the voices, panic and pain. Fuck,fuck,fuck. Someone shouting, screaming, nearby now. Very near. And then the realisation, the awful dreadful face of my father, lying right by me, maybe a metre or two away, his voice distant but terrible, animal cries, tears in his eyes too, streaming down his face, maybe because of the dust in his eyes, maybe because of the pain, because he's lying there, in the dust and noise, gasping, holding his stomach, like the straps and belts and buckles and pockets are holding him together, and maybe they are. A sudden realisation, a shock- this is not a dream. I am really here. This is really happening. An urge, powerful, primal: must get to him, to say something, to hold his hand, to comfort him while he's dying. Yes, I know, I know this is his death, his awful death I am seeing. I don't want to, tried many times to push such thoughts from my mind.

But it's my Dad, and he's dying and he's scared, no, terrified. I crawl towards him, in the dirt beside him, on this dusty road, under the azure blue Afghan sky, under searing heat, through smells like a butcher's shop, and shit and something else, unfamiliar, strong, like a chemical smell. Realise with instant comprehension that I smell the explosive which has just gone off and killed my father, will kill him, has killed him. Does it matter? I am really here now and I can almost touch him. Stretching my hand upwards to reach his: 'Dad, Dad, Dad, I'm here. It's me, Dad, look over, listen to my voice, Dad, it's me, it's Andrew. Dad, Dad?' He hears! He turns his head.

'Andrew?' Desperate hope in his voice. 'Andrew? Andrew?' Suddenly others, by him, soldiers, like him. That one, who came to our house. Saying things like mate, don't worry, a scratch, we'll patch you up, don't worry. But gasps as he looks down, sees the bloody mess where my father use to be. 'Christ, medics, get us a medevac, fucking quickly, fucking bastards. Hang on, mate. Hang on. You'll be fine. Soon have you sorted'.

Others now, looking serious. Someone gives my Dad an injection. Dad's looking round, searching with his eyes and ears. 'Andrew? Andrew? Andrew?' Who's Andrew, someone asked. The other one says 'His son, I think'. He's calling for his son'. And I'm reaching for him, almost there, crawling, taking such a long time, like my legs are made of lead, like I'm not able to move them, inch by inch, the gravel and small stones digging into my elbows and knees as I haul myself forward. Dad, Dad, Dad, I call, hoarse, choked with dust, Dad, Dad, I'm here. Dad, wait, I'm almost there.

'Andrew, Andrew,' he calls.

'It's the morphine,' someone says.

'Andrew!' He sees me! I see him, our eyes meet. I grasp his hand, I can feel him, he grips my hand, I feel it. I feel it!

'My son, Andrew, Andrew. I'm so sorry, so sorry. My beautiful boy.' Tears in his eyes, streaming down his face, he looks at me.

'Don't worry, mate. You'll see Andrew again, don't worry. Where's that fucking Chinook, then? Fuck!'

I'm here, Dad, hold my hand. I'm here to take you home. Don't be scared.

'I'm so sorry, Andrew, my beautiful boy. I'm so glad you're here. I'm sorry I let you down.'

My voice breaking, dust, tears, pain. 'Don't be silly, Dad, you've done us proud. I love you. I love you!' I squeeze his hand, tightly, tightly, never let go.

'I don't want to leave you, Andy. Never did. My boy, my beautiful boy.'

The other soldiers, pushing pads into his stomach, blood on bandages, coughs, his eyes fixed on me. We look intently into each others' eyes, then, nothing. He's gone.

'He's gone, Sarge! He's gone.' One of the others speaking, patting the one I know on the shoulder.

'No!' he says. 'No, no.'

No, I say. Can't you see me? I'm here! He's my Dad! You can't have him. No, no way. Dad! Don't go! But he's gone, gone forever. I hold his hand but the grip loosens. They start to say something else.

'Ambush! Fire ahead-stay low! Landing zone- fuck, fuck! Get outta here!'

More dust, sound of helicopters, sounds like fire crackers, dust, dust, noise. Then I'm cold. Really cold. Cold, dark, then white. White everywhere. Soft, cold, white. Red then, my arm, my coat, red against the snow, blood red on snow white. I look up and see him overhead, glaring, roaring silently into the cold cold night, his iron maw opened in mute majesty, the Maiwand Lion.

CHAPTER THIRTEEN

Angelus

I remember the sounds of bells from nearby St. James's Church drifting across to me from the opposite side of Forbury Park. I remember thinking this is how I'm going to die, right here, looking up at the sky, now clear, black and sprinkled with stars, like the ceiling of Heaven, with him, the Maiwand Lion, like the face of God staring down on me. I did not feel panic or fear just resignation. I knew that my time had come, and I was OK about that. All the pain had left me now and I was glad of the chance to sleep, to sleep, perchance to dream... Strange the stupid things that come into your head when you're about to die. I don't suppose many people get the chance to talk about this, obviously but I remember thinking how Ash would laugh if I told him that I was thinking about lines from Hamlet as I lay dying. Brennan's voice came into my head then, telling me off for lying down in the snow, saying that I had important things to do, and a lot of work to get through if I was to get the grades I needed in the exams. And then Uncle Edward's voice, shouting my name, saying he's over here, over here, I see him, over here. And me thinking, of course I'm here but what are you doing here? And the sound of church bells ringing out in the cold silent night.

The next thing I remember feeling is irritated that some people were trying to get me to wake up. Leave me alone, I just want to sleep, I don't need to get up, it's not time for school, I just want to sleep. But they wouldn't let me sleep. Their hands pulled at me and dragged me onto something and then I was being carried somewhere. I remember the noise of the siren, feeling like I was going to throw up, wanting to get up but not being able to and then from nowhere, her face again, like an angel, Angela O'Rourke, and her voice like honey over velvet, smiling at me, giving out to me in a good-humoured way, saying I was too old to be out playing in the snow at all hours. And then sleep again, interrupted by noises, and movements, and voices and people pulling at me and then quiet. At last, peace and quiet, in a dark place where a small screen glowed in the darkness, blue and yellow and red and numbers flashed saying everything is going to be OK.

And then it was daylight, and I was awake, lying in a room I did not recognise but realised at once was a hospital room. The night before felt like a dream but I knew I hadn't dreamt it. Something very real and very important had happened to me and it was because of the Lion. I lay there thinking through what I'd seen and experienced the night before. I must have been lost in my thoughts as I didn't notice the door to my room opening and only slowly became aware of the face of Nurse Angela O'Rourke, smiling at me as if we were old friends.

'You're awake, good. I just need to take a few more obs from you before I finish my shift. You're looking a lot pinker now than when they brought you in- you were literally blue with the cold. How are you feeling?'

'Good,' I said, and I meant it. I really felt good, like my old self again, like I hadn't felt in such a long time. It was as if whatever had been going on in my head was suddenly switched off. It's like when there's a fridge in the room humming away, you don't notice the noise until it stops and then you realise how loud and irritating an intrusion it had been.

'Can you remember what happened, Andrew?' she smiled while adjusting the blood pressure cuff around my arm. She had such a lovely way with her I felt like just blurting everything out, but of course I didn't. I still realised enough to know that telling her about moving statues would get me Christmas dinner in the Psych Ward.

'Don't really remember much. Just walking around in the snow, climbed into the park, don't know why, just an impulse really, and I guess I must have dozed off or something?' I could feel my cheeks redden at the lie and her eyes told me that she knew I was lying.

'Well, your little snooze in the snow very nearly finished you off. When they found you, you were severely hypothermic. They could barely find a pulse. You're a very lucky young man. A little while longer in those temperatures and.....' Her voice trailed off, there was no need to say anything further. I knew how close to death I'd been, my own and my Dad's.

'Well, let's see if you've thawed out fully, shall we?'

She placed a thermometer in my ear and waited for it to beep.

'Normal,' she smiled. 'You're a proper little Christmas miracle, aren't you?' I shrugged and mumbled something about knowing I was lucky to be alive.

'Listen, Andrew. We've met a few times now. You know you can trust me, don't you? Is there anything going on you'd like to talk about, you know, with you, how you're feeling? I'm happy just to listen, no judgment. And if you're not comfortable talking to me then I can find you someone else, although I hope you feel you can talk to me.' I looked into her kind eyes and thanked her but said whatever had been troubling me previously was over now and that it had been dealt with for once and for all last night. I was better now and would be OK.

She smiled at me again, her face showing she was resigned to the fact that I wasn't going to talk to her, although she'd rightly guessed that I hadn't just wandered into Forbury Park last night on a whim. She touched my hand gently at first, then squeezed it tightly, her face became suddenly serious.

'I know you've gone through a lot lately, Andrew. But trust me, it does get better. And life is wonderful, you know. And not to be taken for granted, especially when it's so fragile. It's a precious thing so take care not to throw it away just because you can't see your way beyond something. Time is a great healer and sometimes events just have to run their course.' She looked at me straight in the eyes. I felt as if she was staring directly into my soul, like somehow she knew everything.

But of course she couldn't know, not really. But I knew then that she was right about what she'd said. And that's what the night before had shown me. Somehow seeing my Dad's death made it more real and because it was real it couldn't be changed, and had to be faced. I knew I had the strength to face it. I knew I would be OK then.

'Your Uncle's been waiting outside for you all night. He was the one who found you. Apparently they'd gotten worried about you when it got so late and you hadn't come home or gone round to one of your friends, especially given the night that was in it, with all the snow. Shall I show him in before I go? Then we can sort out some breakfast for you. Can't promise it will be up to much but it will be warm, at least.'

'Could I have some porridge, please?'

She laughed. 'I'm sure we can arrange that for you.' Then she was gone and soon Uncle Edward stood where she'd been. He looked grey and washed-out, like he hadn't slept all night, which was probably the case. I suddenly felt ashamed, seeing him standing there, looking at me, the worry etched in his face, the puzzlement evident in his frown. But he tried not to let it show.

'Thank God, you're OK.' He forced a smile.

'I'm so sorry, Uncle Edward. All I seem to be lately is trouble for you.' I could feel tears, of shame or regret well up in my eyes. He suddenly rushed forward, and hugged me tightly.

'We thought we'd lost you last night, Andrew. We were all so scared. The important thing is your OK, that's all that matters.'

After a minute or so, he relaxed his bear-hug and sat back on the bed, just talking calmly about things, about how Mum had called him, frantic, saying we'd had a big argument, that I'd run off and that she was scared I'd come to harm. He had tried to reassure her. They'd gone through the list of phone numbers of all my school friends, asking them if I'd turned up at one of their houses. Eventually, just before midnight,

Ash's Dad came round to our house, told everyone that Ash had an idea where I might be but didn't want to say why. That's why they'd come to Forbury Park. But they'd organised a proper search party and everything, with Ash's Dad and the plonker, walking the route I'd most likely taken down by the Thames, while Uncle Edward and Ash drove slowly through the snow down to the park. Ash had found my footprints in the snow, leading around to where I'd jumped the wall. They'd both clambered over the wall to see if they could spot me but at first couldn't see anything. Apparently my footprints in the park had been obscured, as if fresh snow had fallen although they were still visible outside in the snow on the pavement. They split up and each walked a broad arc around the Lion. It was Uncle Edward who'd spotted me, barely discernible, covered by snow. It was red sleeve of my jacket that caught his attention, blood red on the white of the snow. He alerted Ash immediately and told him to call an ambulance. He could barely detect a pulse. He had prepared himself to have to tell my mother I'd died. Tears appeared in his eyes as he told me this.

'I don't think I would have had the strength to do that to her, Andrew. You know how much she loves you, no matter what's gone on between you both. You mean more than life itself to her. When she heard we'd found you, lying in the snow, she asked me, straight out, is he dead? It was like she'd been preparing herself for the news. Well, she was almost right. Another little time in that snow, and quite frankly, we wouldn't be having this conversation. You've got to thank your friend Ash for saving your life. We didn't have a clue where to look for you or even where to begin. He was the one who suggested Forbury Park. He still won't say why and, to be honest, I don't care what the reason is either. I'm just glad he was right.'

Good old Ash. He'd come through in the end, even though I'd rebuffed him by not taking his call that night. His logical mind put two and two together and calculated that the Lion had been the subject of all my recent erratic behaviour so if I'd had another 'episode' he figured that's where I'd go.

'Listen, Andrew. You're mother's in bits over this. Once I knew you were out of danger, I convinced Jonathan to take her home and calm her down, try to get some sleep. She knows things between you both have been difficult. But whatever's happened, she's still your mother and you're still her son. So for my sake, if no one else's, please go easy on her. You might think that she's not suffered grief like you have or even that she's moved on too quickly. But I can promise you, Andrew, she loved your father very much, too much, some might say. And his death was the hardest thing she's ever had to cope with. But everyone deserves a second chance at happiness. Your father had been pushing her away for years before he died. We could all see it. He never talked about things. But I think he was in a great deal of pain. He tried to cope with it by drinking too much but that just made things worse. So your Mum made a brave decision, a few years ago, to put your interests first and that's why she left your Dad. If you'd not been around then she'd probably have continued to try to cope with him. But she could see the damage being done to you. And she always put you first, above all others. And she always will. So, please, whatever's been said and whatever's been done, don't make things worse by punishing your Mum. She's already punished herself enough.'

I felt ashamed again. Uncle Edward never really opened up like this, not to me anyway. He was normally very reserved and avoided all sort of emotional issues if possible. But he was very close to Mum and very protective of her. If anyone knew what she was feeling or thinking, then it would be him. So I had to listen. And I wanted to listen, to forgive, to move forward together, as a family. I realised then that I'd been angry with her for things she couldn't possibly control. I blamed her for not feeling how I did. But how could she have done? We're all different and we all deal with things in our own way. And if we can get it, why shouldn't we try to get something good in our lives, even if that's just someone to talk to or to listen to us.

'It'll be OK, Uncle Edward,' I promised and I meant it.

The rest of the morning was spent being poked and prodded hourly to check I was 'stable' but I knew I was going to be fine. The consultant looking after me came to see me with his team on ward round. He made light of the situation, saying that I'd been found asleep in the snow but had forgotten to build an igloo. Luckily for me, I was healthy so should make a full recovery. He team rhymed off my blood results, including 'tox screen' for drugs and alcohol which were all negative. They asked for a neuro consult given my previous episode in November but seemed relaxed about it. But then came the inevitable psych consult too. I knew to expect this. After all, it's not exactly normal to go to a park in the middle of the night in the worst snow storm to have hit the town in half a century and then go for a little lie down. But I decided not to resist and felt quite calm about it all. After all, there was nothing to fear now. I had experienced the worse thing I could face and lived to tell the tale.

Mum came in with Gran about lunchtime, apologizing for staying away saying she wanted to allow the doctors to do their job. She seemed a bit apprehensive and reserved, not surprising really. The place above her lip where my elbow had made contact was clearly bruised even though she'd attempted to cover it up with make-up. Gran near smothered me with kisses and hugs, saying what a blessing it was that I'd turned up safe and sound and thanking the saints for my protecting me. I reached out a hand towards Mum.

'I'm sorry.'

'So am I,' she replied. That was all that was needed. She pulled herself towards me and enveloped me in tight hug. The smell of the perfume I'd bought for her filled my nostrils. But more pervasive than that was the sense I had of relief flowing through both of us and the return of love between us, if ever it had been gone. Gran started to sniffle back tears. Mum whispered in my ear:

'I'm so proud of you, Andrew. I was so worried we'd lost you. Nothing is worth that, nothing. You are the most important person in this world to me, do you understand? Nothing and no one else will ever come between us again.'

'It's OK, Mum. It's OK. I love you, too. I'm sorry I've put you through all this. I don't really understand what's been happening to me but it's going to be OK now. I know it will be. I want you to be happy. That's what Dad would have wanted, even if he couldn't make you happy.'

Mum pulled out of the embrace so she could look into my face.

'But he has made me happy, darling. He's given you to me. That's the most wonderful thing anyone has ever done for me and I could not ask for anything better. You have his eyes, you know. Bright, intelligent eyes, with just a bit of mischief twinkling in them.' We both laughed a little. I knew she was deliberately avoiding saying anything negative and that was what I chose to do too. What was the point of raking everything up again? What had happened, happened and no amount of regret or recriminations could change it for anyone. Life is precious and we do not get second chances often. But sometimes we do, and sometimes we get to see the value of something before it's taken away from us completely. Other times, we only realise what we've got when it's gone but those times should make us appreciate things more and value the people in our lives even more. It was nearly Christmas by then but the most important gift I could ever be given I'd already received and that was the chance to say good-bye to my Dad and horrible as it was and as unbelievable as it seems, I know that really happened and that I had been able to provide some comfort to my Dad in his last moments and that to me is the most precious thing I've ever received or ever will.

CHAPTER FOURTEEN

Christmas Eve, 2009.

The snow remained on the ground all that week in the run up to Christmas but there were no fresh falls of the magnitude we'd seen on the day I near froze to death in Forbury Gardens. But the temperature remained well below zero, like England had drifted northwards towards Iceland, like we were in the Arctic Circle suddenly, frozen and white. Reading appeared unusually pretty at this time as the snow rubbed out all its usual ugliness. Even I got caught up in the festive mood, once they let me out of hospital, managing to get some last minute Christmas shopping done in town. The shops appeared unusually colourful against the white covering of snow everywhere. I don't know if it was simply due to all the colourful Christmas lights strung between the buildings on Broad Street but everything then appeared to me brighter and lighter, like I had emerged from a long dark tunnel blinking into the sunlight. My mood was good and I was looking forward to a family Christmas, something I would never have believed possible even a few short days earlier.

The hospital had discharged me after 24 hours observation and another round of brain scans and EEGs with a clean bill of health, at least my physical health. There still hung above my head a big question mark about my mental health in everyone else's mind. For my part, I had never felt better but that did not dissuade Uncle Edward from insisting I have another visit with Dr. Medusa. Because of all I'd put everyone through, I didn't feel like I could refuse so I agreed to see her. As luck would have it, she had been able to offer me an appointment that Thursday, Christmas Eve. I was surprised she was working so close to the holidays but then, I thought, she probably didn't have much by way of friends and family to celebrate with so perhaps this was her way of keeping herself busy. But I was determined not to allow another meeting with her to mess up my mood or bring me back down. In some perverse sort of way I even sort of looked forward to seeing her again.

Mum offered to drop me off at Medusa's office, perhaps because she thought I wouldn't go if left to my own devices but I convinced her to trust me and told her I was happy to go on my own. Medusa's lair looked exactly the same as before, down to the old magazines on the coffee table in the waiting room. The only addition was a pathetic looking artificial tree blinking forlornly in the corner. It had seen plenty of Christmases, I thought. And rather than add festive cheer, it reeked of regret and lost opportunities, its lights performing an SOS calling for someone to please put it out of its annual misery. The same receptionist was on duty as before. She smiled in recognition when I arrived to an empty waiting room, asked after my mother and made some small talk about the terrible weather, relating a rather tedious anecdote about how she'd fallen arse over tits when getting off the bus in town because the council had not gritted the footpaths, only the road.

'It's like you don't exist in this country unless you're driving a car,' she complained. 'But even people who do have to get out of them sometimes and use to footpath to get to their final destination, isn't it? So it's in everyone's interest to ensure the pavements are safe to walk on. Just look at my wrist here, it's lucky I didn't break it!' She showed me her wrist, wrapped tightly in a bandage, which appeared dramatically white against her brown skin. I nodded in sympathy, actually praying for Medusa to appear to relieve me from the tedium of this inane conversation.

Soon enough, she appeared, resplendent in a bright red cardigan, trimmed with white faux fur at the collar and cuffs and sporting a novelty Christmas brooch which had Rudolf's nose blinking away on her ample bosom. She looked like Mrs. Claus in the get-up, the mad hair piled up in an untidy bun as usual topping the whole outfit to perfection. I couldn't help but smile when I saw her and part of me thought better of her for making the effort. After all, her job was pretty depressing so it was good that she had a go at raising everyone's spirits. Though from the look of the miserable creature she was showing out from her office, all these efforts were in vain. This was the same woman I'd seen on my first visit. Her eyes were puffy with tears and she dabbed her nose with a very well-used paper tissue.

'This time of year is always difficult for people, my dear,' Medusa comforted her while expertly ushering her out the door. 'The thing is to stay positive and just throw yourself into the spirit of the thing. I mean, time out from the hustle and bustle of life can be enjoyable even if you're by yourself. And it's always nice to have an excuse to eat too many *Cadbury's Roses* while watching *The Wizard of Oz*! I'll see you in the New Year. Do try to have a Merry Christmas, despite everything.' The tone in her voice suggested this was unlikely but everyone felt better that it had been said.

I waited for her to notice me but it didn't take her long, greeting me effusively and saying how lovely it was to see me again. She even offered me a mince pie, home-made, claiming they were rather good, even if she did say so herself. I declined politely, eyeing her mad hair and imagining the likelihood of at least one or two strays finding their way into the mince meat filling, probably supplemented by cat hairs from the large number of moggies with whom she undoubtedly shared her home. She ushered me into her office, cluttered and disarrayed as ever, inviting me to sit on the battered old sofa while she resumed her usual seat, squeezing her big arse back into its well-worn groove.

'Well, then. Let's see, what have you been up to since we last met?' She read a letter she'd picked up from my file which had the hospital's letter head printed on it and remained silent for a few minutes as she digested its contents. Slowly, she raised her eyes to meet mine, removing her glasses from her nose and letting them dangle from the chain around her neck, nestling snugly beside Rudolf on her breasts.

'Another little episode, I see. And with the Lion, again. Looks like you were lucky to get away with this one, Andrew. So do you want to tell me about it, why you were found half frozen to death in Forbury Park last Monday night? '

I decided I might as well be frank with her, to a degree anyway.

'It was just something I had to do, to see it, the Lion, that night. I don't know why, exactly. I just needed to get out of the house and my feet sort of led me there.'

'And did you intend to do an impression of a frozen turkey or was that just an accident, eh?'

'Just an accident,' I repeated, smiling wryly at her. 'I didn't mean to top myself or anything. I guess I fell asleep or something.'

'Or something?' she repeated, incredulity dripping from her tongue. 'So why there, then? Why did you go there? I mean, if you had to get out of the house wouldn't it be more normal to go round to a friend's house rather than set out like Scott of the Antarctic, in the middle of the night, to wind up in a deserted park when it was ten below zero? You must have had a pretty good reason to schlep all that way in the snow.'

'No, no special reason. I just thought it would be cool to be in the park all by myself in the snow...'

'But you weren't by yourself, Andrew, were you?' she interrupted. 'He was there, your friend, the Maiwand Lion, wasn't he?'

'It's just a statue,' I answered sarcastically. 'I'm not some deluded freak. I know it's not real.'

'But the last time we met you told me that you saw it move, that it somehow communicated with you, don't you remember?'

'Well, I said a lot of things, last time. I was only winding you up, giving you something juicy to chew on. I mean, I've seen the sort of people you get in here, complete nut-jobs. I thought maybe I'd try to blend in.'

She leaned back in her arm-chair, exhaled loudly and then seemed to be marshalling her resources, forcing her voice to remain controlled and calm.

'I can see you're planning to play little games with me today, Andrew, and that's fine. I mean, it's your time to spend as you wish but don't play me for a fool. I've told you before that my only interest in working with you is to help you. I know you're a very bright young man and I know you are not stupid enough to try to cover up something important just for mischief. So I'll assume you're not telling me everything because you're afraid of the consequences. Am I right?' I shrugged indifference as a response. So she continued:

'I've dealt with many patients over many years, more than I care to remember if I'm honest. And what I've come to realise is that I cannot help anyone if they do not wish to help themselves. It's taken me a long time to really understand that. I've also learned that people generally want me to help them or else they wouldn't waste their time coming to see me. For some people, I have to play a little game of cat and mouse, you might say, encouraging them to open up by enticing them out of their hidey holes with little titbits of truths that speak to them. So I'm going to throw you a little titbit, is that OK?' I shrugged again but a little more warily, not quite sure she where she was going with this.

'I don't think you are or were suicidal, Andrew but I think you had fallen in love a little bit with the idea of death. And that's not abnormal. Often, when we lose people we're close to we fantasize about seeing them again. This is the basis for most of the world's religions, you know, the conceit that they are still with us, out there, somewhere, just beyond our perception. But the priests and shamans, they convince us that maybe they can indeed commune with the spirits. And they construct rituals and rites to add credence to their actions, to add to the mystery and hence their powers. Are you with me, so far?' I nodded I was but wasn't really.

'In some instances, these priests invoke their powers through the use of special religious artefacts to which they attribute particular meaning. Sometimes even special places are created to allow communion with the spiritual side which we call shrines. At such places, the devoted or deluded, you could argue either side, take their petitions and prayers in the hope that those specials places will enable them to be heard more easily by their ancestors or the spirits, a bit like whispering through a megaphone you might say!' She chuckled a little at her own joke.

'So people have been doing what you've been doing for centuries, perhaps millennia, Andrew. It's perfectly human if not logical. Because it talks to a need we have to believe that those we loved are not gone from us forever. And if that gives us some comfort, then what harm, eh? But if we take things to extremes, then perhaps there can be some harm.'

'But who are you to judge?' I interrupted. 'Religions have provided comfort to people for a very long time and when nothing else could. Look at my Gran. If it wasn't for her faith then she probably couldn't get through the day. I'm not saying I believe like she believes, but I do think there is something other than this world and what we perceive in it. That doesn't mean I hear voices or speak to angels, it just means I am open to things that can't be explained by logic or science alone, not yet, at least. And, as you say, if such things bring people comfort then what harm does it do?'

'And does it bring you comfort, Andrew?'

'Yes. Yes, it does, actually. I don't expect you to understand because I do not understand it myself. I don't know exactly what's been happening to me lately but I know that something has happened to me, and that's been a good thing because it's allowed me to do some things I needed to do?'

'Like what, exactly?'

'Like say good-bye.' The words floated between us for a few seconds. Medusa's face softened a little, and she leaned forward.

'And that's really important, Andrew.' She placed her hand on my arm. Her hand looked younger than her face.

'Yes. Yes, it was, very important. I didn't think it was possible to do it. But he made it possible, the Lion. Somehow, I don't understand it myself. But there are lots of things I don't understand but I accept them all the same. So I choose to accept this, and to be thankful. Because in all this darkness, this one glimmer of light has rescued me. I have experienced something very special and I won't allow anyone to take it away from me because it is good, even if it was hard to bear. And you won't find it in my brain on an MRI scan or an EEG. But it's part of me now, just like the fact that my father is dead is part of me. You can't see the space he's left in my life anywhere but you can feel it. I can feel it. But now, I can also feel that there is something more than we can see with our eyes or touch with our hands. And that's good to know. It has helped me, healed me.'

Medusa looked at me for a while before speaking, smiling when she did.

'Then I'm glad too, Andrew. I'm very happy for you. I can see how different you are compared to when I first met with you. I know you won't believe me, but even I believe in things we can't understand. The difference between us, perhaps, is that I hope someday we will understand them.'

'Me too, actually,' I replied, meeting her smile. 'But for right now, it's not that important to me.'

I left Medusa's office feeling like we had concluded our business together. I wished her a Merry Christmas and I meant it too. I also meant it when I told her I hoped to never see her again. She took it in good part, and asked me to pass on her compliments to my Uncle. I said I would. Then she told me that I looked a lot like him when he was younger. When I asked her how she knew that, her answer nearly bowled me over.

'We were in medical school together, Andrew. In fact, you are very lucky indeed you don't have to call me Auntie! We were once very close indeed. But a different life and a long time ago. Thank god, says you, eh?' She chuckled to herself and disappeared back into her office, leaving me well and truly flabbergasted.

Ash called round to the house that evening. Mum had invited him and his Mum and Dad to a special Christmas Eve party held in their honour to say thanks to them for all their help in finding me. I also told her to invite Jonathan. She laughed when I used his name rather than my usual 'plonker'. Then she hugged me and told me how proud she was of me and the young man I'd become. She told me that my father would also be proud of me. I hugged her back. Everything is going to be OK now, I told her and I meant it. We weren't going to become the *Waltons* or anything, but we were going to be OK.

Jonathan didn't come that evening because he was spending Christmas with his brother's family in Sussex but he did express his thanks for the invitation and I was pleased. We had a full house that evening, with Gran and Uncle Edward, Ash and his Mum and Dad, Mum and me. There were huge amounts of food to eat. Mum must have bought Waitrose out and Ash's Mum brought looks of delicious Indian food as well, all home-made, of course. After a couple of hours, Ash and I sneaked off to my bedroom to get away from the parents and spend some time on-line. When we'd been chilling for a while, I told Ash that I was really grateful for his intervention the other night, and that without his help I might very well not have survived the night. He shrugged awkwardly, saying it was nothing, he just did what anyone would have done.

'But no one else would have thought it through like you did, mate!'

'Maybe,' he conceded. 'But I was just following deductive reasoning, really. After all, if you've ruled out the possible, whatever remains, however improbable, must be true!'

I laughed at his Sherlock Holmes/ Mr. Spock mash-up impersonation.

But, you know what, I really thought about the meaning of that phrase properly that night. I decided that my experience fitted into that category, something improbable but true. Then, Ash asked the question I knew he'd been dying to ask since last Monday night:

'So, what happened the other night? Did you witness something again, with the Lion, I mean?'

I laughed a little at his choice of the word 'witness', as it sounded so Old Testament or something. But I thought I owed him some sort of explanation, even if I didn't want to tell him or anyone else the whole story.

'Yeah, I did 'witness' something, Ash. Something I can't explain and something I won't even try to explain. I don't know if what I experienced really happened or if it's all in my mind but it really happened as far as I'm concerned and it's all good. It's helped me in a way no one else could have done. But I couldn't have gotten through the past few months without your help either, and in a way that's been the most important thing I've realised, that I need my friends and my family.'

'Totally gay,' Ash answered. We both laughed a bit but at least I had thanked him for his help. And that was all that was left to say or do. And like everyone else who's lost someone in a horrible way, I have good days and bad days but even the bad days are important because they mean that my Dad mattered to people, to me. So I remember him, on his birthday, on my birthday, on Remembrance Sunday and at Christmas but mostly when I look at his picture taken with me on my birthday a few years ago one summer, my Dad and me and the Maiwand Lion.

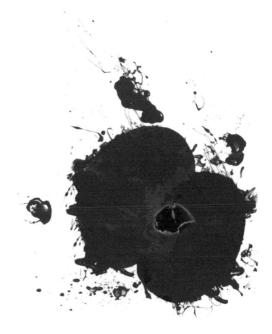

ABOUT THE AUTHOR

ÉJ O'Moore grew up in the shadow of the Cooley Mountains in the historic border town of Dundalk, County Louth in the Republic of Ireland during the turbulent times known as 'The Troubles'. There he witnessed first-hand the cold shadow terrorism casts over a community but also the resilience of ordinary people and their power to overcome hatred and evil. He studied medicine in University College, Dublin and qualified as a doctor in 1991. He currently lives with his partner in Reading in Berkshire, England and works as a senior public health consultant in Oxfordshire and London.

This is his first novel.

Printed in Great Britain
by Amazon.co.uk, Ltd.,
Marston Gate.